THE ALPHA'S ARRANGEMENT (A PARANORMAL SHIFTER ROMANCE)

HOWLS ROMANCE

RYAN MICHELE

1st edition published: July 25, 2017

Editing by: C&D Editing

Cover Design by: Jessie Lane

Izzy needs a fresh start, and moving to the mountains of Montana is just what she was looking for. When she finds the perfect home, she can't wait to begin her new life and get away from the hustle and bustle of the city. Little does she know that her home comes with a surprise.

Carter is known for getting exactly what he wants. When his mate shows up in his small town, the scent of her drives his instincts to claim her immediately. The problem is, she's human and knows nothing about the shifter-wolves that live among her. Treading lightly isn't his way, but he'll do anything for his mate.

He has something up his sleeve to get her in his bed and in his life. Will Izzy resist? Or will she find out that, with the power of an Alpha, she's unable to?

The Alpha's Arrangement is a hot new wolf shifter book sure to melt your ereader. Enjoy!!

CHAPTER ONE

Inhaling deeply, the crisp mountain air flows through my lungs, pure and refreshing. After living in the city for most of my life, coming here is an oasis. There are no sounds of cars, people yelling, or construction on buildings so high your neck aches to look up. Only the flit of a bird off in the distance and something wrestling in the trees can be heard. Peace. Calm.

I came to Spear to get away from the city. It's the complete opposite and beyond perfect. This perfection came at a steep price, though. The old owners wanted to sell, but only for their full asking price. Even with my lawyers haggling, they wouldn't budge, which I admire.

Seeing this place for the first time in person, it's understandable why they didn't want to give up this beauty. I'm not sure I ever could.

The home is large, much bigger than I truly need, but it screamed "home." That's what I need—a home of my own for once. Not moving from place to place, not seeing the world, but having some place steady.

With five bedrooms, six bathrooms, and a full basement,

cleaning will probably be my main activity for a while. The previous owners didn't leave the place a mess, but they did leave their stamp on each room. One that needs to be thoroughly remodeled.

Sucking in one more deep breath, I enter my home, shutting the sliding glass door behind me. Cleaning supplies and food are the top two things on the agenda. The realtor gave me a brief lay of the land after handing over my keys, stating, *"Main Street has everything you need—bakery, groceries, hardware, mechanic, and a couple of restaurants and bars. Not much, but it's enough."* Main street is where I shall go first.

The winding roads from my home into the town make me thankful that I traded in my car for a Jeep four by four. One flick of a switch, and she's ready to tackle whatever comes her way. With the winters, I have no doubt I'll need it. Montana doesn't have light snow normally, and I love that.

Several people walk down the sidewalks on either side of the street, almost giving it a city feel, except there are nowhere near as many people. Their eyes follow me as I move through town, no doubt wondering who the newbie is.

The realtor was definitely correct about the town having everything I would ever need. The grocery store looks quaint, with lit-up windows and people mingling around. Nothing like the supercenters—another great change of pace.

The sliding glass door opens as I enter before grabbing a cart. It isn't lost on me that, as soon as I push my cart through the second door, all eyes are on me. It doesn't bother me. Instead, a smile spreads across my face. I'll never know the people here if there's a scowl on my lips. This is my fresh start. My way of leaving the hustle and bustle behind and finding my happiness.

Coasting down aisle after aisle, I get a lay of the land, giving slight nods to those who stare. It would be nice if they would say hi or something, but that goes both ways.

Smiling, I go back to the canned soups, which I hate, and get the ingredients for my homemade chicken and noodles.

Each aisle goes by in a blur as I collect everything I'll need for the next week or so. Some of my furniture will be delivered tomorrow, and I really want to be a house potato for a while.

I've introduced myself to several more people before I make it to the meat section, when my breath catches. Two mountains of men stand with their backs to me. One has inky black hair, while the other has a lighter brown.

No sooner do I stop the cart and see them, they turn to me in unison, and that's when my lungs become deprived of oxygen.

Both men are gorgeous, but the one with the inky hair calls to me, with eyes that are a deep navy, looking almost black. Whoever his parents are gave him fantastic bone structure, a strong jaw, and a masculine nose. Not to mention his size that is only slightly bigger than the man next to him. The forest green, long-sleeved thermal he has on showcases each dip and valley of his muscular chest.

This town must have a gym, because there is no way these two men look like this without working out ... a lot.

Inky man sniffs the air, and I instantly feel self-conscious, but I dismiss it just as fast. He can't be sniffing me from that distance.

"Hi." I give a soft wave.

"Well, hello there," the brown-haired man says, taking a

step my way, but inky man throws out his arm, holding the other man back.

Brown-haired man's eyes snap to inky man.

"Mine," inky man growls in a deep, sexy as all hell voice. And while I feel that rumble all the way to my core, his word makes no sense.

"Pardon?" I shake my head, dismissing the comment. "Sorry, hi, I'm Iso ..." I stutter, making a quick decision. New life, new name. Isobel is going to stay back in the city. "Izzy. You can call me Izzy."

"Owen," the man with light brown hair says with a smirk, looking between inky man and myself.

I look to the sexy as sin male who is blatantly staring at me, not making any attempt to hide it. Something warm snakes up my body, causing me to let out a shiver.

Damn, girl, it hasn't been that long since you got any.

"Carter," he states firmly and with authority. "McCavitt house?" At least he proves my assumption about it being a small town where gossip is concerned.

"Yes."

"You get all your stuff moved in?" This question takes me a bit off guard, because it's not one of the normal ones I've been getting. *How do you like it here? Where are you from? Why did you move here?* Those are the normal ones. My stuff, not so much.

"Tomorrow."

His stance changes a bit. The once rigidness of his muscles relaxes, yet he carries himself with such authority that, if one wasn't looking, I'm sure it would have been missed. Carter is casual, but very much on alert for some reason, making me a bit nervous. Somehow, he must sense this, because he inhales and some of that alertness disappears, setting me at ease.

"What time? My men and I will come help you."

"That's really nice of you, but the movers will take care of it." Even if that is super sweet of him, there's no way I'd accept that kind of help from a stranger. It's too much.

"What time? We'll be there to help," Carter repeats, and Owen chuckles under his breath.

"What's so funny?" I ask, instead of answering Carter.

"Nothing, Izzy. I'm just happy you came to Spear."

Carter takes a step forward, moving to the side of my shopping cart so he's mere inches from me.

It's my turn to inhale him. The smells of wood, oak, a hint of leather, and testosterone-filled male come through loud and clear. It's an absolutely intoxicating concoction.

"What time?" he repeats yet again, not backing down.

"Ten." My response comes out before I can filter it, as if he's putting a wicked spell on me and sucking me under.

His white teeth make an appearance, and I fully admit that I'm a teeth woman. Something about when they sparkle turns me on. They don't need to be perfectly straight. It's just the color.

Damn.

"We'll be at your place at nine thirty. Do you want us to bring coffee?" A sexy glint comes to his eye.

"Really, you don't need to—"

"I insist. We help our own."

"Thank you, but ..." A single look from him cuts my words off. This one is different than the sexy one he gave me moments ago. This one is determined and leaves little room to no room to argue.

Carter brings his hand up and tucks a lock of hair behind my ear. All I can do is feel each featherlight touch and try my damnedest to continue breathing. Then he brings his fingers to my chin and holds me in place for a moment, almost like he is inspecting me. When he releases me, it's on a sigh.

"We must be going. We'll see you in the morning."

"Ah ... okay."

Carter takes one more look at me before Owen grabs the cart and pushes it off. I note that the only thing inside of it is meat.

CHAPTER TWO

AIR MATTRESSES SUCK. NOT HORRIBLY, BUT I CAN'T wait to get into my bed. One night didn't kill me, yet I can feel it in my back. Unfortunately, the spring chicken I once was, is no more. Not that thirty-one is old by any means, but when I was twenty-one, I could sleep anywhere at any time, waking up refreshed and alert. Now, I need comfort sleep.

When loud thumps come from the front door, I grab my cell to see it's nine thirty. *Crap.*

Flinging off my one blanket, I toss my long, golden brown hair up in a messy bun. It'll just have to do because Carter and whoever he has with him are here. Damn, I thought I set my alarm at least, wanting to brush my teeth before they came. Luckily, I washed my face before I went to bed, so at least my blue eyes won't look like raccoons.

I fling the door open and, just like at the grocery store, my breath catches. Luckily, one hand is still on the door to help hold me up.

Carter stands so damn tall and broad, wearing yet another thermal, this one navy blue, bringing out his eyes.

His jeans hug his hips like they were made specifically for him. His hair is a little damp, but the way it falls around his face is remarkable. Long hair on men never did it for me. For Carter, it does.

There are several men behind him, but my focus is only on one.

"Hey," I greet as Carter's eyes move down my body. It's as if my breasts feel him looking, because my nipples pebble. It's then I remember what I went to bed in, which isn't much. No bra because, who wears a bra to bed? I firmly believe in letting the girls be free. In that decision, though, my nipples stand to attention in the thin spaghetti strapped tank I have on.

Carter's eyes move down, and he heaves in a breath. My legs are long, and with these short as hell sleep shorts on, they probably look like miles. I'm curvy, all tits and ass, so I have no doubt both are on full display.

"We wake you?" Carter asks as he pushes his way through the door and slams it shut, blocking all his men out.

My mouth drops open. "You just slammed the door on them."

"Damn right. They'll see what I do, and it's not for their eyes."

I look down at my clothes and notice exactly what he's talking about. My first instinct is to hide, but I stand tall.

The heat in the room turns up like the gates of hell are at my feet. Each prick of the warmth sends goose pebbles up my skin. Then, when he touches my arm, that fire blazes where our connection is.

My instinct is to pull back, but for unknown reasons, I don't. Instead, I stare into eyes that beam desire and lust. My core tightens.

"I just got out of bed."

With his other hand, he cups the side of my face, making that spot red-hot, as well. I inhale at the touch as he sweeps his thumb ever so softly over my bottom lip. The urge to lick his thumb hits hard. Instead, I concentrate on breathing. Passing out in this moment isn't an option.

He watches intently as he traces my lip, like I'm the most important being on this planet and he only has eyes for me. No man has ever looked at me like this before. It makes my chest compress. The gesture so mundane to some holds so much meaning to me. I feel like I could stay like this all day long.

A thump comes to the door, and Carter closes his eyes. "Baby, get some clothes on so my boys won't look at you."

Clearing my throat, my feet take me back a step, losing his touch. I want it back so desperately, but only nod, and then go to get dressed.

As I'm upstairs, my clothes now on, low growls and laughter can be heard from downstairs. The noise makes the big house seem even more like a home, like a family. Shaking my head from my thoughts, I make my way down the stairs and follow the chatter.

Stepping into my new kitchen, all conversations halt and all attention comes to me. Seven pairs of eyes, to be exact. Each roaming, each appraising, but it's the navy ones that hold me as I give a slight smile.

"Hi, everyone. Thanks for coming. I don't have any ..."

A large man with golden-blonde hair holds up a box of donuts, while a dark brown-haired male holds up coffee. I dart toward him, needing my caffeine fix, so damn happy they got me a cup of joe, too.

"Thank you!"

A growl comes from behind me, but the brown-haired male just smiles.

I turn to see Carter standing there.

"Did you just growl at me?" I ask, sipping the brew.

Instead of answering, he says, "Boys, outside and wait for the truck."

"They don't have to go outside," I argue. It's not freezing out, but it's not the warmest, either. "At least let me meet the guys who are helping."

I turn back to the brown-haired man who was holding the coffee. "Hi, I'm Izzy."

"Gar."

I make my way through the men and note that someone's missing. "Where's Owen?"

Carter's nose flares. "He had to work."

"Yeah," Jack, one of the men, grunts, and Carter's focus goes to him.

"Now, outside and wait."

All six men move from around the kitchen island where they were standing since I have no chairs yet, and out the door.

"That wasn't nice."

Once the door clicks shut, I watch as Carter's body visibly relaxes. His shoulders lose a bit of their tension and the lines around his eyes soften. It's as if having me away from all his men gives him calm, which is totally preposterous to even think. I've seen the man twice. There is no way my presence would do this.

He moves so quickly until he's in front of me, his hand on my arm, sending tingles in its wake. "You're absolutely beautiful, Izzy."

Some of my steam from his rudeness evaporates at his kind words, and I feel my face softening. Then the door swings open.

"Where do you want this?"

That breaks whatever Carter and I had, but it keeps me busy for quite a while so I don't have to think about the way Carter makes me feel. The want that burns so deep for the man I just met. Directing the furniture is my escape ... for now.

CHAPTER THREE

THE HOUSE IS A HOME. WELL, IT'S GETTING CLOSER TO a home with my furniture in place. With all the men, it only took a couple hours, not even long enough for me to pull out all the stuff I bought for sandwiches for the guys to eat.

As soon as the last box was placed in the kitchen, all the men left. All except for Carter, who's been unrolling glasses and mugs, setting them in the cabinet. After that, he moved on to the plates and silverware, to which I needed to direct him on where things went. The funny thing is, I didn't know where they went, just made it up along the way.

"You don't have to stay, you know," I tell him as we finish yet another box. He's been here for hours without his guys; surely, he needs to get going to do something else rather than help me unpack.

"I'm good," he responds, opening another box and pulling out my toaster. I direct him to the counter by pointing. "What are your plans while here?"

"I'm not sure. I need to get my computers up and running, and WI-FI going for my work. Other than that, relax."

He pauses, his brows coming together in thought. "Why do you need computers to work?"

"I'm a software designer. I create new programs or alter ones already in use to suit my clients' needs."

"Come." He takes my hand and leads me to the brown leather sectional couch where we sit. "And you can do all that from up here in the mountains?"

Happiness fills me that he's curious about what I do. I love it and can talk about it for hours. The last guy I was with told me it was geeky, and he didn't want to hear another word about it, so I didn't mention it. "I can do it anywhere I have a computer and WI-FI. It's the best part of my job."

He clasps his hands. "I take it you like it."

"Absolutely. It's challenging, and I'm good at it."

He puts his knee on the couch, facing me, and I mimic his stance, garnering his full attention. I suck it up.

"What do you do?" I ask.

A sexy as hell smile rolls over his lips. "A business man. Run my family's company."

"Doing ...?" I encourage him to continue.

Carter smirks. "We have several businesses that we keep in line. The bakery in town is one that we own, as well as one of the diners."

"Ah, so the donuts were a because-you-had-them thing."

He leans over and grips my leg. "No, it's a we-were-hungry-and-thought-you'd-like-them-too thing."

"It was nice."

He gives me a squeeze then releases me as a knock comes to the door.

"Who in the world is this? I barely know anyone, and it's like Grand Central Station here."

I make a move to get up, but Carter says, "I'll get it," holding out his arm for me to sit.

"Really ..."

"Really." His tone is curt, forcing me to listen.

He comes back with Owen on his heels.

"Hey, Owen."

"Hey, Izzy. Good to see ya." He's so easy going.

"Same. You missed all the fun," I joke, not missing the tension between the two.

He chuckles. "Place looks good."

Carter clears his throat.

"Right." Owen reaches into his pocket and pulls out a manila envelope.

"Everything there?" Carter asks.

"Yes."

"Go," he orders rudely.

"You don't have to leave, Owen. It's okay."

Carter's eyes shoot to mine as he comes back and sits on the couch. "Now," he growls to Owen, who gives a chuckle and a flip of his hand.

"You really need to be nicer to the people around you. They're all going to walk away one day if you keep treating them like that."

"No, they won't."

I let out a frustrated sigh, looking at the envelope in his hand. "What's that?"

"Something that we need to discuss."

"Since we just met yesterday, I'm not seeing how we'd have anything to discuss, Carter." Curious, yes. Very much so.

Carter pulls out some papers and hands them over to me.

"Care to explain why and how you got these?" I ask, looking

at the front cover of my contract for this house that was signed on the dotted line yesterday. I didn't even think the lawyers got it yet to file appropriately, let alone for Carter to have a copy.

"Because I got a copy, too."

I sift through the pages, noting my initials—I.B.—on the bottom of every page. "Why would you get one?"

"Because I'm part of the arrangement."

Surprise flares in my eyes as my heart picks up a thumping pace. He's so wrong. My lawyers or my realtor would have caught that. There's no way.

"Wait, what arrangement?"

"The house and me—package deal."

"Right, so you want me to believe that these papers"—I hold them up, giving them a shake—"contain a section that says, 'hot guy comes with the house for free?' No. Not buying that one bit. One of my people would have caught something like that. Not to mention how crazy that is."

He leans over and takes my hands in his. There's still the spark, but the ease from before is a little more difficult to find.

Carter squeezes, getting my attention. "There in black and white. Read it."

"Where? Show me."

Only then does he release me and sift through the papers, pulling one out. I look at the bottom first to see if my initials are on it, and they are. Then I take the paper from him.

Upon agreement to reside in said above property, you agree that Carter Masters will reside with you in the home. You will cohabitate for eternity.

There is no way that I'm going to "cohabitate" with a man I don't know.

"This wasn't there when I signed the papers. Is this some crazy joke, Carter? Because, I'm not laughing."

"It's not a joke. It's an agreement. You and me."

"Why on earth would you even want this? I mean, *for eternity*? What's that about?"

"Exactly what it says."

Dumbfounded, I just stare at him, wondering where I fell off the loony train and into this world.

"You don't even know me. I mean, whoever bought this house was going to spend eternity with you? Seriously? You can't be that hard up for a date."

He chuckles. Yes, chuckles.

"Not hard up for a date. And no, if it were anyone else, not a chance in hell."

I shake my head, trying to compute what he's telling me. It's not working.

"So, you had this put in the contract before you even met me?"

"Something like that."

"I don't understand this, and I know I didn't sign anything that states we will be living together for the foreseeable future."

"Go get your copy of the contract and we'll compare them."

It's a good idea, but hell, I can't believe I'm even entertaining this—any of it.

Getting up, I go upstairs to my bag that was tossed in my closet. Not waiting to get down to Carter, I thumb through the documents and stop dead.

Holy shit.

It's there, in black and white, and I signed it. How did this get missed? There's no way my lawyers saw this. I pay them exceptionally well for me not to get screwed on things. They'll be paying for this big time.

Climbing down the stairs, Carter meets me at the bottom, a sexy grin on his face. "I see you read it."

"We'll get it amended. I'll have my lawyers draw up the contracts and get this taken off the house."

He steps closer, getting well into my space. I can't step back because the stairs are there. Plus, the smell of him over-whelms me.

"Give me a month. Thirty days here with you. After that, we'll talk about amending the agreement." Carter inhales deeply, rubbing his nose along the tip of mine. It feels so good that tingles go through my arms and my stomach clenches.

"Why would you want to do this, Carter?"

"Time will tell." He leans over and kisses my cheek. "As much as it pains me, I'll leave you tonight. But tomorrow starts our thirty days. I'll have the guys bring my things, so make room, baby."

"Carter, this is so ... wrong on so many levels. How can you want to do this?"

"Time will tell. Get some sleep." With that, he turns and leaves.

I fall to the steps, elbows on knees.

What the hell just happened?

CHAPTER FOUR

A HOWL WAKES ME FROM SLEEP. IT'S CLOSE, REALLY close.

Curious to see my first sign of wildlife, I move to the window, searching for the sound, when it happens again. This time, though, it feels like it's coming from below me.

Looking down, a gorgeous, black animal stands at my back, sliding glass door. He howls again, directly at the door.

Interested, I make my way down the stairs then freeze when I see the animal. It's not a dog. No way is that thing a dog. It's huge, standing about as tall as I am, his paws way bigger than my hands. His coat may be a beautiful black, but it's his teeth that he licks that gets my attention.

"Good boy," I coo, not knowing the first thing about wolves and if he can hear me or not. It must be a wolf or some crossbreed that I've never heard of before. I knew there were animals in these mountains, but hell, this thing is enormous.

I take a step back when the animal growls, vibrating the wall and the glass, the only thing separating us.

The wolf must sense my unease because it suddenly

goes down on its belly, resting his head on his front paws. It still watches me, but makes no sound.

Looking into his eyes, a momentarily pause hits me as the navy blue catches my attention, but I dismiss it quickly.

"I'm going to head back to bed, big guy. You take a little rest."

A low growl comes from him as he paws the door.

If he thinks I'm opening that door for him, he's sadly mistake. There's no way I'm going to end up being his next meal. However, if he could break through the glass or wanted to, he could have already done so.

"Night, big guy."

I turn on my heel and race up the stairs, hearing him howl. Shutting and locking my door, I then rush to the window and look down at the back deck. The animal is back to lying down, a soft whine coming from him, almost making me want to go back down and open the door. Almost. Instead, I crawl into bed and sleep eventually over-takes me.

By seven a.m., I'm on the phone, leaving messages for my lawyers and realtor who don't answer my calls. If they don't call me back soon, I'll be making more phone calls. Not only that, I spread the contract out and go through the pages one by one to see if there are any differences in any of them, coming up with nothing.

There isn't enough coffee on the planet at this moment to calm me. It's nine a.m., and I've called both of my guys twice again. Each time, the damn recording played, and each time, I lost my cool just a little bit more. They made damn good money on this transaction, and I want some answers.

A loud bang comes to the front door, and for the first

time, I wonder what's wrong with the doorbell. I know the house has one, but all that people do is bang.

As I make my way to the door, there's a moment of hesitation. Carter could be behind that door, ready to move his things into the house, with his guys backing him up. If he moves his things in here, how in the world will I get him out when all of this is straightened out?

I inch backward as the banging starts again.

"Izzy, open the damn door," Carter demands. The sound of his voice sends a pulse of warmth through me. There's no denying the man has me on edge, but I can't let him in without figuring out what's going on.

A tap on the sliding glass door catches my attention, and I turn in a *whoosh*. Owen stands there, hand on hip, huge smile across his face.

"Open up, Izzy. He's not goin' anywhere until we unload his shit."

"No." My answer has him chuckling.

Suddenly, Carter is standing next to Owen, a playful expression on his face, like he knows what I'm doing and reading my mind, which is impossible.

"I need to get ahold of my people and straighten this out," I say through the door. "I'll get it sorted and have my lawyers contact you."

"Izzy, open the door." Carter's eyes penetrate me, compelling me to open the damn door.

Inside, I war with myself, knowing it's a bad idea, but thinking bad ideas aren't so bad.

Damn.

I find myself slowly making my way to the door and unlatching it.

"You really shouldn't move anything in, Carter. As soon

as I get this ironed out, you'll have to leave, so there's no point."

Owen chuckles as he steps through the door, goes to the front, and unlocks it. The same guys from yesterday start coming into my house with boxes and furniture.

"Holy shit," I whisper.

Carter wraps his arm around my waist and pulls me to him, causing my body to slam against his with an "*ooph*." He brings his lips down on mine, and my treacherous body gives in immediately. He tastes all masculine, and as our tongues dance, the passion begins to fire red-hot. I wrap my arms around his neck, pulling my chest against his, and he lets out a low, deep growl, causing my core to tighten.

"Al—Carter, where do you want this?" Owen's voice breaks through the fog this man puts me in, and I pull back immediately, the warmth of embarrassment washing over me. I'm a thirty-one-year-old woman who just got caught making out with a man I don't know.

Carter growls louder this time, making the hair on my arms rise to attention. "Master," Carter responds, turning back toward me.

Looking at Owen, I see he has boxes labeled *bedroom*. "Wait! He can have the guest room down the hall."

Owen chuckles, shaking his head, and moves away without taking my words a bit serious.

"Carter, you're not sleeping in my room with me."

With his hands behind my back, he presses me deeply into him, negating the small distance I had put between us with my jump back movement. He skates his nose across my cheek then our noses touch. My breathing comes in shuddered breaths. There's something happening here. Something serious. Something crazy, considering a man I just met is moving in with me and part of me, deep down, likes it.

"No sense in havin' them do double work. You know, as well as I do, your bed is going to be mine. May not be tonight, maybe not tomorrow, but someday ... soon."

A full-out shiver racks my body. I know he feels it because he smiles.

Crap.

"Anyone ever tell you that you're cocky?"

He smiles.

"And persistent?"

Smiles wider.

"And ...? And ...?"

"Knows what he wants, and that's you, Izzy." He drops his lips down on mine again, and thoughts drift from my brain, leaving the wonderful sensations of his lips.

CHAPTER FIVE

When the pot boils, I dump the pasta inside then give it a stir. Steam comes up in the process. Meanwhile, Carter slices the bread on the kitchen island for the garlic bread. We've been in comfortable silence for a while now. It's different, unique, and I hate to admit it, but I'm loving it. All of this is seriously strange.

I've tried calling both the lawyers and realtor all damn day. It's like they both went on an extended vacation. Not even their secretaries are picking up their office lines. Their cells, nothing. It's really pissing me off, and if I have to track them down, so be it.

Moving to the counter, I slide the buttered garlic to Carter, who takes it then spreads it over the bread. Watching him work is like an art. Each movement calculated, precise, and with definite meaning. He's agile and quick.

With his men earlier, he was demanding but respectful. Every single one of those men showed him the utmost respect, doing exactly what he said.

"Are you Owen and the other guys' boss?" I ask,

needing to know the dynamic there. Not everyone would take orders like that.

"Something like that. I told you of our businesses. Everything goes through me."

"So, are they your employees or family?" Why this comes to mind, I'm not sure, but I'm curious.

"Family."

"Like, your brothers or cousins? Uncles?"

He finishes the last piece of bread and tosses the knife into the bowl in front of him. "Pretty much."

"But you didn't introduce them as your family."

He shrugs. "It's just how we work."

The pot on the stove begins to overflow with bubbles. "Crap."

Carter holds out his hand to me. "I got this." He moves over, pulls the butter out of the fridge, and puts a dollop in the pot. The bubbles recede.

"Is there a wolf issue out here?"

He turns sharply to me. "Why do you ask that?"

I move to the cabinet and pull out the plates, setting them on the counter. "Last night, a huge wolf came to my back door." I look him in the eye. "It howled then growled at me. Luckily, he didn't come through the glass door, but Carter, it could've in a heartbeat."

"Did it scare you?"

"Well, yeah, at first when I saw its size. I mean, I'm not kidding, Carter, it was as tall as I am." He listens as I speak. "But the animal must have felt my fear because it laid down and even gave me a little whimper. Then, when I told him I was going to bed, he growled again, but it wasn't mean; it was more of ... This sounds crazy."

"No, keep going. More of ..."

"Like he didn't want me to go upstairs to bed. When I

got to my room, I looked down and he laid down on the deck, whining. Isn't that weird?"

"There have been lots of wolf sightings. Some calm and nice like the one you saw, and others you need to be more cautious of. A big thing to look for is if they fall down onto their bellies and give you no threat." He reaches for my arm. "Not saying you need to be free with the wolves because some aren't supposed to be in these woods, but that's far and few between."

His touch is electric, short circuiting my brain.

"You know a lot about wolves."

"You have no idea." Carter gives me a squeeze then moves off. "Need to make a call," he calls out as I watch his tight ass move.

After dinner and light talk, we're sitting on the couch, watching a reality show on singers trying to win money, when a tap comes to the door. I look over the couch and give out a small screech. A large, light brown wolf sits on the other side of the sliding glass door. He's on his belly, his paw coming up to tap on the glass.

"What the hell?" comes from my lips as I scramble to my knees. "Another one. This can't be normal."

"Come on," Carter says, holding out his hand for me to take.

"Where?"

"Trust me."

Trust him. *Trust him.* Oh, hell. I know I need to start considering we're living under the same roof for the time being, but this ...

I tentatively lift my hand into his, and Carter pulls me up. We move to the door, his gaze trained on the large wolf.

"Carter, this is close enough." I tug my hand back, but he doesn't release me.

He turns, looking directly into my eyes, determination and something else lingering behind them. "I swear to you, I'll never let anything happen to you. Ever."

My breath catches and my heart palpitates because I believe him. I truly do, yet have no reason to.

"Okay."

"Okay." He turns us back toward the animal, who's still lying on the deck, his eyes practically glowing.

Carter reaches for the door handle.

"You're not opening it!"

"Trust me," he says, while my blood pressure skyrockets.

Carter is opening the door to a wolf. A huge, wild animal.

Holy shit.

He slides the door open, and my assumptions of the wolf jumping at us are totally wrong. Instead, the animal tips his head and looks up at us, not moving another muscle. It's like he's waiting patiently. *A wolf can wait patiently? Who knew?*

Carter snaps his finger and the wolf moves. I jump back, but Carter pulls on my hand. I steady my body as the wolf crawls on its belly, inside the door, into my home, and stops at my feet.

The urge to run hits me hard. My heart feels like it's going to burst out of my chest at any moment.

Carter kneels next to the wolf, who doesn't move again. He lifts his hand and begins to pet the wolf. I almost jump out of my skin, telling him, *"No, don't!"* but I keep my body still, just in case the wolf decides to attack.

The wolf gives out a low whine, but I don't think it's in pain.

"Kneel down here and give him a rub."

"Carter, this has to be the craziest thing I've ever done. Ever."

Carter smiles, one I haven't seen before, and I wish I could tell what it means. "Come on, Izzy."

Thinking and thinking, and thinking some more, I slowly kneel on the floor.

"Go ahead," he encourages.

My hand shakes as I reach out. The wolf doesn't make a movement, which doesn't help the thump inside of me. Its hair is soft, unbelievably soft. A low rumble comes from the animal, but it doesn't move, so neither does my hand. Over and over, I stroke him, keeping away from his face.

"Wow," I whisper in amazement. "Are all of them like this?"

"No."

This makes me pause. "What?"

"Not all wolves are like this one. Some aren't meant to be in Spear, but those won't come to your door."

"How do you know that?"

"I just do." Carter rises, and the wolf's attention goes to him, his snout rising.

I pull my hand back.

"Time to go," he says and, like magic, the wolf doesn't stand. Instead, he scoots back the same way he came in.

Carter closes the door and locks it.

"What about the black one?" I ask out of curiosity.

Carter stares me square in the eye. "Never worry about him. He'll never hurt you."

I'm not sure what to think. How can Carter be so certain? He's confident in a way I can't describe. It's like every word he says is law and he knows it. Can he really make it so? Some part of me, deep in my belly, believes he can.

It makes me feel crazy.

———————

GETTING a glass of water in the middle of the night isn't my normal, but when a hunk of a man wearing nothing but pajama bottoms is two doors down from me, it's hard to sleep. He kissed me so deeply before he went to the guest room that I was pretty sure I'd pass out, just from the touch. Then I laid there, tossing and turning, aroused beyond belief. I could have relieved the ache, but Carter might have heard.

Scratching comes to the glass door, and I jolt, turning to see the black wolf from the night before. He's down on his belly, just like the light brown one was earlier. Carter's words ring in my ears. *Never worry about him. He'll never hurt you.* Do I trust it?

The wolf gives a low whine, and just like before, my body reacts with anxiousness.

Ever so slowly, I move to the door and unlock it. With trembling fingers, I then slide the door open, taking a huge step back.

The wolf slowly crawls to me, head down. Once it gets to my feet, it stops.

Letting out a huge breath, I kneel next to him, lift my hand, and move it toward his body. Slipping my fingers into his fur, I feel that it's softer than the brown wolf's.

The black wolf lets out a few whimpering sounds that almost sound like comforting ones.

Continually, I sift my hands in and out of the wolf's hair, the animal not moving a muscle. I find this odd comfort wash over me, tingles forming in my fingertips. I study the animal beneath me and am enthralled.

"You know, you're a beautiful creature," I begin talking to him. "Sorry I was scared of you last night. I've never had a wolf come to my house before, let alone seen anything as big as you. Except for the brown wolf." At the mention of the other wolf, I feel a rumble and pull my hand back. "Easy there, big boy." The wolf begins to calm, and I go back to stroking.

"Don't tell your friend, but I'm a bit fond of you. Wish I knew why. Maybe it's your eyes. You remind me of someone." My focus goes to the stairs before turning back to the animal. "This is very strange, big boy. Never thought in a million years I'd pet a wolf, let alone two in one day. And this arrangement ... it's crazy—living with a man I don't know for eternity. There's no way that can be correct. Maybe I should have stayed in Jones Bend." I continue stroking. "I feel a weird connection to you, and I don't understand it."

We sit there for a long time; me randomly talking, him letting out a few noises, but nothing that scares me to the point I pull back.

I watch as he sniffs the air around me. Brave or stupid, I haven't decided yet, I let him have my hand to sniff. When he licks me with his rough tongue, I pull back, startled at first. Then he lays his head back down and all is calm again.

Eventually, I can barely keep my eyes open. I don't want him to leave, and it saddens me that he has to. When I tell him it's time, he goes without any growling. Then, when I look out my window from my bedroom, he's gone.

CHAPTER SIX

"WOMAN, THIS IS A CRAZY AMOUNT OF COMPUTERS," Carter tells me as I hook all my monitors up in my office. He's not wrong, but for what I do, I need six monitors and more cables than should be deemed legal. It's a good thing I understand it and love my job.

Since he's right, I keep quiet, hooking up the machines.

"You gonna leave enough room for my desk?"

I look over to the corner where his desk, bookshelf, and single computer sit. It's good the space is pretty large, but still ... "You may want to move your stuff to your room."

He lets out a laugh. "Not happenin'."

Shrugging, I tell him, "Suit yourself."

He goes to his desk, making his own space, and we work in comfortable silence.

At lunch time, he makes us sandwiches, which we eat out on the back deck. I've noted his cell phone rings a lot. He takes the calls outside of the room where I can't hear. I'm not too sure how I feel about that. I have no right to be jealous about anything, but he does kiss me, give me soft touches, and is exceptionally attentive to me. When I asked who he was talking to, he told me his guys, and I let it rest.

I came here for a fresh start. Suddenly, I have the home of my dreams and possibly the man of my dreams in a package deal. Carter pulls at something inside me, he gives me comfort, and as much as I wonder what he does, who he is, I find that I don't want him to go away.

For an awkward arrangement, one I'm still not sure about, I find myself becoming settled in it.

"Shouldn't you be working?" I ask him after we finish eating.

"Took the week off. Wanted to spend it with you."

"Why?" I sigh. "Carter, this isn't adding up. I can't get ahold of my people. The contract is there in black and white, and I have no idea why you would want to live here with me."

Carter rises, pulls me up from the chair, then his lips are on mine. He takes and takes and takes, demanding more of me with each movement. The kiss consumes me as I fully give in to it, in to him. He sucks all the breath from my lungs, and when he pulls away, I'm a bit light-headed.

"Because, we're gonna take this time to get to know one another."

"Normally, people do that without signing a contract saying they have to live with each other."

"One thing's for certain, Izzy; I'm not normal."

You can say that again.

That night, he cooks steaks on my back grill, baked potatoes, and corn on the cob. His meat practically mooed it was so pink, but he ate it all. Carter made mine medium-well, and it was divine. We spent another night on the couch, this time watching movies. Carter changed it up on me, though, by holding me tight.

"I WONDER why the light brown wolf hasn't come back," I tell Carter over breakfast a couple days later.

"What do you mean?"

I realize I didn't tell him of the black wolf coming to me at night. He has every night since the first. I've even made it a mission to make sure I'm awake so we don't miss our time together. I even had this silly notion to let him sleep in the house instead of the cold outside, but I didn't let into it. He's a wild animal, after all.

"The black wolf has come every night, but the brown one hasn't."

"Do you want the brown one to come?" His question has a hint of suspicion.

"Well, not really. Not like I like the black wolf coming around, but still, if he's nice, I don't mind him hanging out with me."

A low growl comes from Carter.

"Did you just growl at me?"

He says nothing as he goes back to his pile of bacon and sausage. The man can seriously pack on the meat. His body doesn't show an ounce of it, and the more he doesn't wear a shirt, the more I don't want him to wear one. Like, ever.

I drop the growling questions and the conversation.

"WHERE ARE YOU OFF TO?" Carter asks, coming down the stairs.

My mouth waters at the sight of his sculpted body. It's something I've only read about in books. Which reminds me, I need to find the box for those and unpack them in my office.

"I'm running to the realtor's office to see what's going on." I've left messages over the past four days and I'm over it. There is a possibility the man went on vacation or something for the week, but not even his secretary is answering the phone when I was able to get right through before. Something is up, and I need to figure it out.

He stalks my way, lust burning deeply in his eyes. When he reaches me, he encases me in his arms and attacks my lips.

He tastes so good and kisses even better that I fully give in to the feeling.

My core clenches and gives a slight spasm. Carter growls like he felt that movement, clutching me tighter and pressing my breasts tightly to his hard chest. It's my turn to groan as he takes the kiss deeper, tilting my head.

Carter begins to move us as a haze of desire washes over me, taking me to a level I haven't ever been on. One where the want is so deep that it scorches my insides and the throbbing ensues.

In the haze of need and desire, the realtor and this arrangement is forgotten. All that remains is Carter and our connection.

I'm tipped over and laid on the soft couch, Carter's hard body coming down on top of me and pressing me into the cushions. He roams his hands over my body as he settles his hips between my legs, his hard length resting against my core through his jeans. Tingles and then pulses course through my core and into my lower body.

I reach inside Carter's shirt, skating my hands over his hard, muscular back. Up and down, my nails score him. This does something to him, like igniting a switch. His hips start to move, his cock hitting my clit. The pressure becomes too much, and I have to rip my lips away from his to cry out.

The orgasm is right there, on the cusp, and I reach for it. Beg for it. I want it with everything inside of me. Having Carter here these past few days has been a test of will, and since grabbing my vibrator hasn't been an option, I need this. I need to be unwound.

"Carter," I moan, beginning to move my hips in time with his. He moves his lips down my neck, scoring his teeth against the sensitive place between my neck and shoulder. He stops moving his hips, though, so as good as it feels, I can't get over.

"What do you want, Izzy? I'll tell you exactly what I want."

"Please." The word is breathy. Turned on isn't in my vocabulary at the moment. More like on fire.

He brings his lips to my ear. "I'm going to eat your pussy until you scream."

"Oh, God."

He smirks. "Not God. Carter."

Carter tears my pants and underwear from my throbbing body, not one bit sweet or slow. He dives between my thighs, licking me from bottom all the way to top, stopping at my clit as it thumps, demanding attention.

Carter nips my clit hard as he sticks two fingers inside of me, filling me and setting off my orgasm. My hips buck up, back arches, and chin lifts as I yell out my release. However, he doesn't stop. Each touch of his tongue is like a thrashing, as if he can't get enough of me and I surely haven't gotten enough of him.

Out of breath, I look into his navy eyes and watch them smolder. Something about seeing him between my legs with that expression sends another bolt of lust through me, dampening my pussy further.

"Shirt off, Izzy."

With shaky arms, I do just that while he strips out of his clothes. My core clenches at the sight of him, and a low moan comes from my lips.

He removes his shirt and his body is perfection personified. Sculpted abs look like he works out rigorously, and the V that dips down into his jeans is so fierce I just know that what's under those pants is something that will wreck me. Sure enough when the pants come down, he's hard and ready.

I know I shouldn't have sex with him, but damn, my body craves him like a drug. Never have I wanted a man this badly before. Like, if I don't have him in the next few minutes, I'll combust.

Carter straddles me at my waist, not putting weight on me. He then places his hand around his very hard, long cock, stroking it up and down. His grip is strong and fierce, and a damn huge turn on, increasing my desire for him.

When I bring my hand up to touch him, he releases himself then positions his hand on top of mine, squeezing him hard, harder than I would have done myself. He shows me exactly what he likes until his head falls back. Meanwhile, it's taking everything I have not to squirm from the heat building inside of me again. I love this. Love that he does this to me.

"Press those tits together, Izzy."

I do as he instructs, and then he spits down on his cock before moving the hard length between my breasts. He grips my flesh and presses them together hard, creating a channel for his dick, then proceeds to fuck them, back and forth, shaking the couch.

The tip of him comes close to my lips, so I stick out my tongue and taste him. This spurs him on, and soon, he's coming all over my chest and chin.

Still hard, he moves back down to my core and feasts on me.

"Fucking love seeing me on you, marking you." His words rumble against me, sending just the right amount of friction. Then, when he latches on to my clit, I implode, this one much more intense than the first. I scream his name.

He inserts his fingers, pumping me toward another orgasm. My back falls as it wrings every last drop of my energy out of me, which is disappointing because I want more.

Carter drops his body on top of mine, his come sticking between us. Looking into his eyes, I see so much swirling inside of them. I wish I knew what he saw in me, because I feel my heart constricting for this man. I feel like there's a connection building with these invisible wires connecting us, and it scares the shit out of me.

He kisses me, and I wrap my arms around his neck.

When he pulls away, my heart squeezes. I pull him closer, not wanting this moment to ever go away. We stay like this, staring at one another for so long he begins to embed himself inside me, and that scares the shit out of me, too.

CHAPTER SEVEN

Pounding hits the door, and Carter's up, moving toward it.

Since Carter sidetracked me this morning with hunting down the realtor, I've tried calling him again to no avail. Sad thing is, I was a bit happy he didn't answer. If he did and Carter and I had to nix this arrangement, I'm not sure how I feel about that at this point. Especially after our time today.

I really thought he was going to have sex with me. When I asked why not, he said, *"Izzy, when I take you, I take you mind, body, and soul."* That sent goosebumps all down my spine. The words were so complete, so real, I felt they meant so much than their outward meaning. Even more, I liked it ... too much.

Carter is more of a gentleman than his rough exterior lets on. He's no teddy bear, that's for sure. Maybe the big bad wolf, with a nice side. I laugh at the thought. *Wolf.*

Loud talking comes from the entry, and I get up to see what's going on. Carter's guys all pile into the house. Several are carrying grocery bags, moving into the kitchen.

"Hi," I say on a wave and get smiles and nods as they pile in and dump the bags on the kitchen island.

"Hey, beautiful," Owen says, smiling.

"Hey, what's going on?"

Carter comes up beside me and wraps his arm around my shoulder, pulling me into his side. This makes Owen's grin wider, while heat floods my cheeks.

"Al ..." Jack looks over at us and shakes his head. "Carter, we just came to hang out."

Upon his words, it hits me. They missed him. He's taking his time away from them to be with me. It's sweet and must mean that he really does want to be here with me.

I feel myself leaning into Carter, who kisses my temple.

"Coupla hours, then you're out," Carter decrees, smiling around the room.

Throughout the night, Carter's eyes barely leave me. I feel them like sharp daggers that turn me on mercilessly. I've learned that Carter lives at a place called The Den with all the men, plus more. This totally boggles my mind, and I set it aside to remember to ask Carter about it later.

Maybe he knew about this arrangement before and never had a place of his own. Maybe it's normal for men to be arranged into a home—and therefore, a woman—like this. It's all strange, but somehow, for me and Carter, it seems to be working.

Carter and his family have a very good relationship. They fire quips back and forth, and Carter burst out laughing several times. Each time, I can't help watching. I make it my mission to make him do that with me.

They're all close, and I'm happy that Carter has that.

The guys say they need to talk, so Carter takes them out to the back deck. Exhausted, I go up to my room. Lying in bed, I think to myself that I hope they don't scare my wolf away tonight. Seeing him is a light in my life I love. Regardless, my eyes drift shut and I fall sleep.

My body thumps and my core throbs, waking me from a deep sleep. The room is pitch-black with only a small bit of moonlight coming through the windows. Tempted to put my fingers between my thighs and work out my aches, I refrain, wanting to see if my wolf is back.

I get out of bed and look down through my window, feeling an ache deep in my chest. He didn't come.

Disappointed, I head down to the kitchen in search of a drink, hoping that maybe, just maybe, my wolf will come. Listen to me, *my wolf.*

My breath catches at the sight before me upon entering the kitchen. Carter stands with his back to me, hands resting on the kitchen island and head down, reflective as if he's deep in thought. His back is a sculpted work of art, the planes and rivets so perfect it's as if a Greek god decided he needed to be exquisite.

He tips his head to the side, a grin on his face. "Hey, Izzy."

"Hey." I pull myself out of my thoughts and grab a glass, filling it up from the tap then taking large gulps. None of it cools my raging libido one bit.

His heat hits my back as he moves his strong arm around my waist. Nuzzling my ear, my knees go weak. My neck is so damn sensitive, but with him, it's ten times more so.

"Can't sleep?" he asks into my neck.

"Needed a drink."

He blatantly sniffs my collarbone all the way to my ear. "It better have been me you were dreaming of." Carter latches on to my earlobe, sucking and pulling. He has to take on more of my weight as I feel my body begin to tremble. "Was it? Were you dreaming of me, Izzy?"

"Yes." The word is breathless as his assault on my tender flesh continues.

"You know you don't have to sleep alone."

I groan, not wanting to, not one little bit.

"I bet I could make you come, just like this." He sinks his teeth into my flesh, not enough to draw blood, but enough to give me a pinch. My core clenches and a spasm hits my clit.

"I think you could," I respond, gripping the kitchen counter.

His nips get harder. "I *know* I can."

Arousal flushes me. I'm in dire need of a release.

"Come to bed with me," I whisper, turning in his arms and latching my lips to his.

He picks me up by grabbing handfuls of my ass. I wrap my legs around his hips and my arms around his neck. We move, but don't lose contact of our lips. Each step he takes rubs my pussy against his hard length, heightening everything around us.

My back hits the softness of my bed, and then his weight comes down on top of me.

Carter doesn't have sex with me, but he does give me three orgasms that rock me to my knees.

CHAPTER EIGHT

WAKING UP IN CARTER'S ARMS IS THE BEST FEELING ever. I've had lovers before, but not one made me feel the way Carter does. None of them. Ever.

After kissing me slowly and making me come again, Carter decides he is taking me out for the day, so here we sit, in his huge truck, looking over a wide-open field full of trees, flowers, and tall grass. It's breathtaking. The sun hits it just right and casts a beautiful glow emanating through the tall trees to the ground below. It goes on for acres and acres, and the only way I can tell is because we are on a hill, overlooking it all.

When he told me he was taking me to one of his favorite places, I'm not sure what I was thinking, but a huge field out in the middle of nowhere wasn't on the top of the list. Maybe a diner or where his family lives. Here? Not so much. It's gorgeous, don't get me wrong, but for a man's man like Carter is turning out to be, this didn't register on my radar. I keep learning new things about this man every time I turn around, and all of it, I like.

"This is beautiful, Carter."

"My family and I come here often."

"For picnics or something?" There doesn't appear to be a flat ground or tables anywhere, but I'm sure they could get creative.

"Something. We do eat here. Run around. Spend time with one another." It makes me miss my mother back in Jones Bend. I need to call her and get in touch.

"That's nice."

We get of the truck and sit in the grass. I rest my head back on his shoulder while the cool breeze caresses my face. There's a sense of calm, of peace that's magnified here. I thought I had it at my house, but here, it's times ten. A house up here on this hill, looking over this field every day, would be paradise.

"We've been doing it for generations, handing it down throughout the years. It's important to me to keep the tradition alive."

"So, you own this?"

He chuckles. "Yes, me and my family own this."

"How far?"

"As far as your eyes will take you, then add about thirty more miles."

"Wow, that's ... just wow." Impressive doesn't even cut it. No wonder the place looks like it's well taken care of in a way that screams his family honors it.

I've never had something like that. My mother moved us around often after my father passed on. That's why coming to Montana was so important. I wanted that stability and not have to move.

Out in the distance, tall grass and flowers begin to move. A gasp leaves my lips as I see my brown wolf and another lighter brown wolf. I try to sit up, but Carter pulls me back.

"Carter, my wolf."

He growls. "Not yours. Black is yours."

Damn, that man can read my mind.

"Okay, the other wolf that came. Do you think he knows we're here? And where's *my* black one?" I emphasis *my*, hoping he gets the point. Black is mine, no matter what, but brown is sweet, too. Not like black, but still.

"I'm sure he's around."

The wolves lift their noses and begin to sniff the air. Even this far away, their eyes come directly to us.

"They smell us," I whisper as the brown wolf lets out a howl. Not a scary one, but one almost like he's calling someone or giving a code of some sort.

"Yes, they do. Are you scared?"

"No," I whisper, watching the two wolves who begin to move our way. "They're coming."

He says nothing as we watch.

My heart leaps in my chest as other wolves begin to come out of the grass. Mentally, I count up to sixteen of them.

"Holy shit, Carter. There's almost twenty of them." They're so large and strong, but still pretty far away as they walk closer. "Do you think we should get out of here?"

"Are you scared?" he asks again.

I feel my heart thumping in my chest faster and faster. "A little. With just two, I didn't feel it. But twenty? They could really hurt us."

"And if I told you they wouldn't, would you believe me?"

My breaths come quicker as they get closer. "How can you be so sure? They're so big."

He tightens his arms around me, and I feel my heart begin to slow. I have no idea how it's possible, but it happens. The calm isn't there, but some of the fear dissipates.

"Trust me, Izzy. I swear, nothing will happen to you. I'll die before that happens."

He'll die? Holy hell, that's a doozy of a proclamation to give someone. If he's wrong, I guess we're both goners.

"Now, you need to relax. They can sense when you're scared, and you'll lose the power you have over them. They want confidence and to know they can trust you, just like you can trust them. It's a give and take relationship. If you show that you're scared or fear them, they won't trust you, and it won't work."

There are so many meanings inside of what he said that it takes me a bit to pull my shit together and do as he says. Of course I'm scared. There are twenty wolves coming my way, but I also don't want to ruin the relationship I have with the brown wolf, or hell, the black wolf, if he shows up.

Pulling up my big girl panties, I take a huge breath and slowly let it go. I gravitate toward Carter's strength and feed off it, knowing he'll lead me.

Carter must sense this because he says, "Good girl," just as the wolves get closer.

My brown wolf sniffs the air then hunches down on his belly, coming closer a little at a time until his head is mere inches from me.

I reach out and pet his fur. "Hey, bud. How've you been?"

One by one, the other wolves do the same. Each of them go down on their bellies and each lay their heads down on the grass.

"You're right," I say softly to Carter.

"Yes. They like you, and you like them."

For the rest of the afternoon, I watch as the wolves play

together. There is growling and biting, but it's not ever angry. It's comradery, a family. Sometimes, one will run off while a couple of others chase it and bring it back to the group. Other times, they will find rabbits or some other small animals and chase them. I thought for sure that one of them would eat what they caught, but surprisingly, they didn't. It's as if they want me to like them and are afraid that, if they did so, I'd be scared. Truth is, I want them to. I want to see them be natural and do what they normally do, so when I say, "Get 'em, boy!" it turns into a chase with several little bunnies not making it. Not that I'm a fan of killing rabbits, but it's what wolves do. I wouldn't want them to come in and dictate how I live my life, so why would I do that to them?

Each wolf takes their turn coming up to Carter and I, allowing me to pet their heads. Some even lick me, which I take as a good sign.

The entire time, Carter stays by me. We talk, laugh, and have an overall wonderful time. One that I will cherish forever.

When I ask if we can come back, he readily agrees.

When we leave, several of the wolves whine, and I swear I see some tears forming in a couple of their eyes. Not that that's possible. Is it?

That night, Carter's family comes over once again. It feels right. It feels like home. Carter feels like home.

When they leave, I curl up against Carter for the night and don't wake up once. Not even to see my wolf.

CHAPTER NINE

For five days straight, Carter and I get up and go to the fields. And I find myself putting off calling the attorneys and realtor, wanting to spend more time with Carter.

Everything is perfect—going to the fields, coming home and having dinner, then going to bed in Carter's arms. The only thing that can be better is if Carter took the step to have sex with me. We fool around and each get off, but he's holding back. Every time his veins pop out on his neck and muscles strain, it kills me, but I don't know why he is. It's something we need to talk about. That's what I set out to do over breakfast.

Making my way down stairs, the smell of bacon frying has my stomach growling. One thing about Carter is, the man can cook, and boy, does he eat.

As we sit at the table, I ask, "Why do you hold back on me?" I don't want to be that self-conscious woman, but it unfortunately is a bit hard. I'm practically throwing myself at him, yet he refrains. I know I'm not hard on the eyes, but Carter is drop dead gorgeous with a personality to match.

He could have anyone. Anyone. So, why me and why hold back that part of himself?

"What do you mean?" he responds, popping a piece of bacon in his mouth.

I push my plate back and rest my elbows on the table. "We kiss, we touch, but you don't take it any further. Why? What's wrong?"

He rises from the table, scoops me up bridal-style, and moves us to the couch where he sits me on his lap. "Nothing's wrong."

"But you ..." I start, but he places his finger over my lips, stopping me.

"Let me finish."

I nod, and he removes his finger.

"I need to know you're ready to hear me and be open to everything I say."

A pit begins to form in my stomach at the uncertainty his words leave behind. Not him; he's very certain. For me. Am I ready to know whatever this is that's implied in his words?

My feelings for this man are growing each day we're together. Simple touches he gives me while walking by me in the kitchen send my heart aflutter. If this is a barrier between us, then I want to know. I want to figure out if what we have is just lust or if it's something that's buildable, lasting.

"I'm open."

He kisses me softly on the lips. "When we get to the field today, I'll tell you everything. You trust me, right?"

"Yes." He's never given me any reason not to. Even with the wolves, he proved his knowledge of them. There is definitely trust there.

The drive out to the field is quiet. I'm not sure if it's me or him, but the tension is so thick. I hate it because it's never been like this.

When he reaches over and squeezes my hand, I know it's me. I'm the one feeding the monster.

I let out a huge breath and focus on the man beside me. His loving touches. The way he is with his family. The way he takes care of me. The way he helped me move in. The way he's right about the wolves. How he says he'd die before anything happened to me. All of it flitters through my thoughts, causing a bit of the tension to seep out.

When we get there, he opens my car door, holding out his hand, which I take. We've sat in the same place every day. I find comfort here as Carter holds me and we look out over the field. No wolves in sight yet.

"Talk to me," I whisper, cutting through the quiet.

He tightens his arms around me. "What I'm about to tell you cannot be shared with anyone. Ever. I'm trusting you with it."

I nod in agreement.

"I'm a wolf-shifter."

My body jolts as my mind skips a few times. "A wolf-shifter?"

"You know I'm not going to beat around the bush. I'm going to be straight with you. My family and I turn into wolves, and then back into human form. The wolf you've seen—the black wolf—that's me."

Shock doesn't even cut it. So many thoughts roll in my head as I try to pull away from him, though he doesn't let me, so I say, "Please, I need to look at you for this." He releases me, and I turn so I'm facing him. "You want me to believe that you shift or turn into a wolf? Like the movies?"

He chuckles. "Those movies are shit. But yes, I can turn into a wolf."

"Are you okay?"

"Yeah, baby, I'm fine. The best way for you to know is for me to show you." He begins to rise.

I swallow, knowing the next words out of my mouth are some of the strangest ever. "Wait, you're going to change?"

Carter takes off his clothes, making me hot as he does, which is crazy considering he just told me that he shifts into a wolf.

I should run, right? I should take off and pray I get away.

The fear builds, but it's like I can hear Carter in my mind, soothing me and telling me that I have to be fearless to keep their respect.

I fight to breathe and calm myself.

"I'll never hurt you, Izzy. Swear it on my life."

Stunned, all I can do is nod and watch.

Carter removes his jeans and underwear, and I gulp at what's between his legs. I've seen it, played with it, had it in my mouth, but every time, it puts me in awe.

"Izzy, there's no reason to be scared."

That's when it happens. He rocks my world on its axis.

Carter's body changes. His face elongates as his nose forms a snout, his black covered furry ears standing up to attention. His body sprouts fur as he develops paws with very sharp claws and lands on the ground with a thump.

I jump up and back, not knowing what the hell to think. The black wolf—*my black wolf*—gets down on his belly, paws out in front of him, head down on his paws. He looks up at me, and that's when I realize it's Carter's eyes staring back at me.

My knees crash to the ground. "Holy crap, you're a wolf." There isn't fear there, just wonder and amazement.

Carter's wolf crawls over to me, setting his head on my lap. Lifting my hand and putting it on his fur, he gives a low growl, but it's the same one that Carter gives me when I do something he likes.

We stay just like this for a very long time, me petting my wolf, knowing that deep inside there is Carter. Knowing that the man I'm living with shifts back and forth between human and wolf. Not knowing what in the world I'm going to do next.

A rustling behind me has me turning and Carter standing up, getting in front of me, protecting me. The brown wolf and the twenty-something others from the past few days all come out.

Carter shifts back immediately, and I hear his bones breaking and twisting. That has got to hurt.

Soon, a very naked Carter stands in front of me, hands on his hips, ass turned my way. Damn, it's a fine as hell ass.

"Shift!" he orders, and suddenly, my mind is blown again.

One by one, the wolves in front of me turn into humans; my brown wolf turning into Owen.

"Holy shit," I breathe, taking in their forms, their very naked forms.

"Cover up," Carter orders, and hands go to lower regions, while the women cover their breasts, yet Owen has a cocky smile.

I take a step back and my feet falter. As I'm heading down on my ass, Carter shows up quick as a flash and grabs me before I hit the ground.

"You're a wolf."

"Yeah, baby."

"But, I thought those were only on TV and books."

"Books?"

"Yeah, I read books about shifters all the time. Wolves, panthers, tigers, lions ... and more."

Carter growls, "Only animal you have is the one holding you."

"I just ... What does this mean?"

Carter turns to the other wolves. "Leave."

Silence hits as they move farther away from us. Part of me is sad to see them go.

Carter sits in the grass with me on his lap, staring up into his beautiful eyes.

"What this means is that you're my mate. This is why I haven't had sex with you. I want you to know exactly what you're getting when we do."

"I feel like there's more to this you're not telling me."

He smiles. "Love that you're so damn smart."

I say nothing, just continue to stare at him, waiting for some answers. Lots of them.

"Wolves have a very keen sense of smell. When we met in the store, you instantly hit me, and I knew you were my mate."

"How?"

"It's in our blood to know exactly when the one shows up. It's like you have a place embedded deep in my soul, my heart, and my brain. When I inhaled you, there was no question."

"But how can I be your mate, lover—whatever—if I'm not a wolf?"

"According to the Ancients, one's mate can be anyone—human or wolf. You happen to be mine."

"So, what does this mean? I'm your mate, so we start officially dating or something?"

A grin plays on his sexy lips. "We have been 'dating' for a week now."

My mind reels as I play back the past week. He's right. It may not be a traditional way of dating, but still, we've gotten to know each other, he's made me fall for him in several ways, and I love his damn wolf. Tricky man. Or wolf. *Shit.*

"So, you planned this? The house with you contracted with it?" I narrow my eyes at this thought as fire bumps through my veins.

"To an extent. Knew you were my mate, knew you were human, and I needed a loophole in the contract. In doing that, since we met after you signed the contracts, we had to do some calculated maneuvers with the paperwork."

"What?"

"The contracts you signed first didn't have the arrangement clause in them. It was after the fact. We replaced those and the ones you had in your closet."

"I knew it!" Relief floods me because I read that damn thing several times and didn't see Carter as part of the deal. Surprisingly, it doesn't piss me off like it probably should.

"I had to get to know you the human way, because the wolf way would have scared the living shit out of you."

"What? How?" I feel like a damn broken record as I keep asking questions, but I need answers.

"If you were a wolf, I would have taken you outside at the store, threw you in my truck, and taken you away from prying eyes. I would have mounted you, bit you, and we would be mates."

"Wait. Mounted me? Bit me?"

"Yes. The traditional way to take one's mate is from behind, in human form. Then I'd bite your shoulder, sealing us together for all eternity."

"Holy shit."

"With you being human, it'll be different."

I say nothing; just sit there in stunned silence.

"Once we consummate the mating and I bite you, you'll go through the change."

This jolts me. "Change?"

"You'll change into a wolf."

"What?" I screech and quickly move from his lap. "You want me to turn into a wolf?"

He sighs deeply, standing up. "Would I love for you to? Yes, because that means we'll be side by side for hundreds and hundreds of years. I'd love to have you by my side. I need to have you by my side."

"Wait. What happens if I don't agree to this?"

His face turns solemn. "Then that is your decision, and I'll go away."

"What happens to you?" I begin to pace back and forth, the grass crunching below my feet.

"You don't need to worry about this."

I stop at his words, my eyes turning into slits. "Tell me."

"I'm Alpha of my pack, the leader. Since I know who my mate is now, it changes things. If we do not become full mates, my power will slowly diminish. Therefore, someone from my pack will eventually challenge me. When they do, I have to fight to keep my position." His eyes fill with pain. "But chances are, I'll be weakened to a point that I'll lose. It's fight to the death, Izzy."

I suck in a breath, my hand coming to my heart as it beats erratically. "You'll die?"

"Eventually. We all do at some point, anyway, Izzy."

"This is too much. Way too much."

"I know, but you need to know this is the reason I haven't taken your body. Once I do, Izzy, there's no going back. Ever. Wolves mate for life. There are no divorces. The only thing that separates mates is death." There's a bit of trepidation in Carter's tone, as if he fears I will turn this all down.

My mind whirls as I try to process everything he's just laid out on the table for me.

CHAPTER TEN

I LAY IN BED ALONE, MISSING THE WARMTH OF CARTER, but needing space to allow myself to think. I feel as if Carter has thrown my life in a blender and pushed the speed button, grinding everything up inside me.

Wolves. He wants to bite me and make me one forever. For hundreds of years. Carter seems so sure that I'm the one for him, but how on earth can he know that he won't get sick of me in ten years and push me away?

I've seen many divorces and bad breakups. He says it's for life, but that's what marriage vows say, too. That doesn't mean that people don't go their separate ways every day.

My feelings for Carter have grown so strong over the week, and having him away from me just this short amount of time is tearing at my insides. It's as if there is a magical cord connecting us, and the longer we're apart, the stronger it tries to tether us together. It's creating an ache in me so deep that I don't know how to handle it. If I go to him, will this go away? Is this a sign that I'm supposed to be his mate and become a wolf?

Scratching comes to my door, but I ignore it.

It comes again. And again. And again.

Finally having enough, I fling the covers off and open the door to see my black wolf—Carter—sitting there.

With a heavy sigh, I tell him, "Come on, boy."

He follows me into the room as I climb back into bed. He perches himself on the side of the bed, our faces aligned. He's a gorgeous animal.

He lays his head on the cushion of the bed, and I reach over to pet him.

"I can't believe you're a wolf, Carter."

The animal whines. No, my Carter whines.

"Carter, change please," I whisper, and instantly the wolf recedes and a very naked Carter stands before me, going down to his knees.

"I couldn't stay away." He reaches out to brush the hair away from my face. The touch is so gentle, and I feel those cords pulling us together tightly. "Do you feel that?" he asks.

"What?"

"Don't deny it, please," this big, strong man pleads with me.

I can't deny this or him. "I feel it."

"That's the start of the bond between us. It's only going to get stronger as the days go on. Imagine what this will feel like in a year, ten, or a hundred. I want this with you. You by my side, me by yours, until our dying days."

"That's one hell of a marriage proposal, Carter."

He smiles, taking my breath away. "I'm down on my knees, baby."

My heart squeezes and those strings get tighter. I want to be with him. Even as strange as all of this is, I want this.

"Come here, Carter."

"Izzy, if I get on that bed with you, I'm not going to be able to control myself. Now that you know, I want you now more than ever."

Without a second thought, I respond, "Come and take me."

"Really?"

"Yes, Carter. Make me yours."

His lips devour mine, the connection between us building with each pass. I get lost in the sensations, passion, and the all-consuming bond we have forming. It's like those invisible strings are twisting and turning together with each kiss we set on each other's lips.

The build is swift as he moves his hands up my shirt, pulling it off in one swipe.

"No panties. Let's make this a rule from now on." He doesn't allow me to answer, his tongue already inside my mouth, doing delicious things to me.

Carter pulls away and flips me on my front. "Need to claim you, then we'll go nice and slow."

Trepidation hits as second thoughts cross my mind. Do I really want to be a wolf? Do I want to live forever? Do I want to be tied to this man for the rest of my days? Yes, I do.

At that thought, the worry floats away.

On my hands and knees, he massages my ass. His grip is strong and demanding.

Two fingers dip into my core while his thumb circles my clit, hard, rough, and controlling. Then a finger or a thumb enters my backside, sending a new trill of sensations through me.

He plunges in and out, and I thrust back on his hand, fucking myself hard. His fingers easily move through my wet folds.

While part of me expects him to continue to play, I'm

surprised when he proves me wrong by removing his fingers then plunging his cock inside of me in one deep, long stroke, touching parts of me he has yet to claim. He's definitely going to claim them tonight. I fall forward on my elbows from the force, my head falling down.

He's so deep inside me. I can feel him everywhere. Something sharp grips my hips, but I can only focus on the in and out thrusts of Carter inside of me. He's so powerful and intense.

Carter wraps his hand around my hair and pulls me all the way up so my back is to his front as he continues his brutal thrusts. In this position, I feel him in other ways, hitting new spots and sending me so close to the edge. His hips are like pistons, moving so fast that the bed shakes.

I don't just feel him in my body. I feel him in my heart, as well.

"Rub yourself. You need to come." His voice is rough and sexy as all hell.

I reach down and do what he asks, sending off a series of shocks. It hits hard and fast. I keep rubbing my clit, continuing the orgasm.

As I ride the wave, I feel his teeth sink into my flesh at my collarbone, causing another orgasm to crash through me. This one is different. This one, I don't just feel euphoric from it. No, this one is magical. That connection I've felt with Carter solidifies, and I can feel everything about him: the thump of his heartbeat, the intakes of his breath—all of it. It's like there are wires connecting Carter and I. Bonds that can never be broken.

He shoves his cock inside me, stilling, as he growls his release.

We stay there for long moments, both of us needing a reprieve.

He smooths his tongue over the bite as I fall to the bed, out of breath and out of energy. Carter falls next to me as his come drips out of my body.

"I don't feel any different," I tell him, still out of breath, but still me.

"You'll start to go in heat. That'll last for a few days before your wolf will show."

"Heat?" As soon as I ask the question, I know exactly what he means, because my body throbs, aching with the need to come. It's a burning desire that is almost painful.

"Yeah, heat." He kisses me, already knowing exactly what I'm going through.

He takes me again ... and again ... and again, until I finally pass out from exhaustion.

THE ACHE GOES AWAY for a brief amount of time, and then comes back with a vengeance. It's as if the world is playing a very cruel joke on me—giving me the best sex of my life, yet causing me pain, as well. I'm all for a little pain with pleasure, but this is just ridiculous.

I get off on Carter's cock, and not five minutes later, I want to be back on it. No, I *need* to be back on it because the burn becomes too much.

Carter tells me not to fight it and that he's at my disposal, which is nice in some twisted, fucked up way.

Each time I come, something inside me shifts and changes. Every time Carter and I come together, our connection grows. It's more than marriage. It's inside us, building and structuring itself into an unbreakable bond. I'm starting to understand what Carter said about never getting a divorce. With the way I'm feeling, I could never imagine not having the man beside me in my life.

We've been at this sex thing for three days now. I never in my life thought I'd say this, but I need a break from the sex. Problem is, I can't. The changes happening inside of me are preventing it. Sleep is a luxury right now that only happens when I pass out. Carter, though, he's always ready to go. Always there doing what he needs to. Taking care of me. Loving me. That's what matters.

He matters.

My body aches in need, but looking at Carter's sleeping form, I roll away from him in bed. The man has been giving me everything, so five minutes won't kill me.

Making my way down to the kitchen, I fill a glass of water and chug it back.

Arousal warms my lower half, and I have to hang on to the countertop to balance myself. Breathing through it dulls the pain a bit, but not by much. Never would I have imagined that my life would consist of me changing into a sex-crazed wolf. The thing is, all I ever wanted was to be happy and with Carter, and now I am.

I can't help being curious about what my life will be like on four legs instead of two, or running in the woods. Will my senses be heightened? I've always heard that animals have a great sense of smell and eye sight. Hopefully that will get passed on to me.

There are so many questions. I probably should have asked before agreeing to be Carter's mate, but when it comes down to it, the pull to him is too strong. There really wasn't a choice in the matter. He is it, and my gut knows that. It just took my mind a bit longer to catch up.

As I think of Carter, my mate, the bite mark on my neck tingles, and my need drives me once again.

The burn intensifies to the point of pain. My knees buckle, and I fall hard to the floor. With a groan, I rest my overheated body on the kitchen floor, loving the cold tile as it helps lessen the heat thumping through my body. I roll my forehead along the floor, hoping for some relief there, as well.

I should have listened to Carter instead of coming down here, but hell, it feels like I've woken the man up every few minutes. This has really been the first time we slept. However, as I lie here on the floor, groaning, I wish I had. I wish I would've nudged him so he could help me take care of this. Now I'm all the way in the kitchen, and I'm not sure I'll make it up the stairs to get to him.

My breathing increases as my insides contract and release, each time harder than the one before. Sweat pours from my face onto the floor as I wrap my arms around my waist. This is surreal—being in this much pain because of an orgasm. And it doesn't stop. Carter reassures me it will, but that moment isn't now.

Footfalls come from the stairs.

"Izzy?" Carter calls.

"Here." I hate that my voice is so damn pained, but there's no masking it.

The steps become louder.

"Shit." Carter scoops me up into his arms, the tightness of his hold providing a small bit of comfort. "Told you to wake me up, baby."

"You were sleeping."

"Hence the *wake me up* part of the conversation."

"It hurts," I groan out as he sits on the couch and moves me to straddle his lap, my core burning. He was right about the no panties and how they'd get in the way. Luckily, I listened to this bit of advice; therefore, he slides right inside of me and the pain instantly dulls.

"I think we'll just stay exactly like this until it passes."

Carter chuckles, but I find nothing about this funny.

When he grips my hips, picks me up, and slams me back down, all thoughts dissipate. The only thing I can do is feel. And Carter makes me do that, repeatedly.

CHAPTER ELEVEN

"Carter?" I call out, tapping him hard on his arm as we lie in bed. I hate that I have to wake him, but this pain I'm experiencing is different.

"Yeah?" His voice is groggy.

"Something's happening to me." Inside my head, there is a push and pull, like it's warring against itself. Each thought is like a lead bullet in different parts of my brain. Holding my head in my hands doesn't help. The ache between my legs isn't like it was before. Now it's my head that's the problem.

"What's wrong?"

"My head ... It hurts bad."

Carter reaches over and grabs his phone. I want to yell at him for making a phone call at a time like this, but then I hear his words.

"Doctor, get to the house now. She's changing and needs meds." He clicks the phone off then turns toward me. "He'll be here in five minutes. You're changing, Izzy. He'll give you something to help. I promise you'll feel so much better in a little while."

I groan, hoping like hell he's right.

Soon, the doctor is there, checking me out and giving me meds. Whatever he gives me instantly helps the throbbing.

"Where were you when all the sex was happenin'?" I quip.

The doctor chuckles, but it's Carter who speaks.

"No one comes near my mate when she's in heat. Ever."

"Will I go into heat often?"

"About once a month, sometime twice, depending on how fertile you are."

"Great," I groan.

"Baby." Carter's eyes burn inside of me. "Swear to you, you'll love being in heat. Get past this, and you'll crave heat every minute of the day."

Thinking of my time of the month, and the fact that I'm irritable and bitchy, I'm sure he'll rethink this quickly.

That's the moment it happens. The moment where my life is forever changed. The moment where I change.

Fur sprouts from my body as I go from two legs to four. As I look, everything is strange. Carter is a bit green tinted, but I notice everything in the room is. I'm not in my body anymore, and this scares the living shit out of me. I'm an animal. How in the hell does this happen?

Under my paws—yes, paws—the carpet feels soft. This is happening so fast, and I'm confused as to what I should be doing.

"Izzy?" Carter asks.

I walk up and lick his chest, letting him know I'm here. Paws are so much different than legs. I almost feel more stable with them.

There is no pain. There is no tension. There is nothing, but freedom, and I love it. Inhaling, I think about how I was right about the heightened smell. Carter's is unique, and one my wolf really loves. The doctor's scent is okay, but not one I crave like Carter's. I can smell food downstairs. Not only that, I can hear really well. There's a drip of water either downstairs or outside. Everything is heightened and beautiful.

"Izzy, switch back," Carter orders, and I growl at him. Yes, growl!

If I could laugh in wolf form, I so would.

He repeats himself several times, but the last time is in a tone my wolf won't deny. It's dominating and demanding.

Slowly, my wolf recedes, and now in human form, naked and on all fours, I stand quickly, covering my exposed body.

"Why did you do that? I liked learning the world through her."

"You have plenty of time to do that. I had to make sure you were in control of your wolf. That you could call her back and change. I didn't tell you that some wolves don't have that change, and when they don't, they stay in wolf form forever. I needed to make sure you'd come back to me."

"Forever?" Forever as a wolf scares the daylights out of me, making me want to rethink this changing thing. To be an animal forever isn't an option.

He reaches over and pulls me in his arms. "Yeah, forever. But you're in control of your wolf. How do you feel?"

"Fantastic. Probably better than I've ever felt in my life."

"That's because you heal now right after something happens to your body. It's the power of being a wolf."

"Wow." This is amazing.

Before I can relish in that, though, my core starts to burn once more. Not as intense as before, but like a calling, wanting its mate.

"Doctor, you can go now," Carter growls. He must have smelled my arousal.

"Let me know if you need anything," the doctor says with a smile, leaving the room.

I hear him go out the door and shut it. Then, I pounce, tearing Carter's shorts off his body in one swipe. I'm amazed at my strength, but I don't take the time to revel in it.

Both of us naked, I push my man down and place him inside me. Then I begin to move.

My entire body feels different. The way my hair hangs down, I can feel each little brush on my back, only it's magnified. Each touch is amped up, and the arousal is off the charts. The intensity of the feelings falls over me, rushing me and making me quiver.

"This is hot as hell, babe, but you've had your fun for days. It's my turn." With that, Carter flips us over, his weight pushing me into the bed while he roams his hands over my body, our kisses becoming frantic. So much so, I don't know where his starts and mine stops.

He's demanding, controlled, and I love it.

"Lie back," he orders as he rises. The cool air of the room hits me, only making my body burn more.

He brings his lips to my core, the heat of his mouth overtaking me. Then he pushes his fingers into me, and with that, combined with this tongue, I combust, exploding in a sea of colors behind my eyelids as I repeatedly scream out his name.

Carter kisses up my body, wrapping his delectable tongue around my nipples. Then his teeth join in for a tug.

My back arches off the bed, wanting more, and I lace my fingers through his hair, holding him to my body.

"Carter." I breath as he moves his way up my neck, taking long moments to lick, nip, and suck.

Closing my eyes, I enjoy the feel, taking it all in. Each time his lips touch me, it's intensified from before.

His lips come to mine, taking me in a deep kiss that we fight for control of. He wins, and I don't give a shit.

"Give me that pussy."

My already parted legs tremble. "You want it, come get it," I taunt.

In one solid thrust, Carter's inside me, causing a low groan to leave my lips. His eyes stay connected with mine as he pumps in and out of me, his cock causing wonderful sensations inside me.

He lifts onto his knees, still keeping his eyes on me, and uses the force to press inside me harder and faster, never relenting.

He brings his fingers to my clit and rubs it fast and hard, the sensations spurring on my orgasm as it hits. Then I scream as Carter comes down on top of me, his lips covering mine and muffling the cries. He picks up speed with his hips as he groans out his release.

He lies his weight on me as he breathes out heavily, and I wrap my arms around him. Only moments later, my body is primed and ready to go again. He obliges.

Over and over again, all through the night, my craving for him doesn't sate. If anything, our bond is tighter. If I could have him inside me for the rest of my days, I'd be happy.

It's as if my body craves this man on a higher level. And damn, do I love this feeling. This connection that I thought was strong when I was a human, is nothing compared to the connection we have now as wolves. It's cemented. Never going anywhere.

Knowing he'll be by my side no matter what, no matter the problems we face, is better than I could have imagined. I love that I'm able to have this with him. I love him.

CHAPTER TWELVE

"It's time for you to come to The Den to meet everyone," Carter tells me at the breakfast table.

For the past three days, we've been exploring this newfound wolf inside me. Sex is out of this world amazing. Walks outside are so vivid and breathtaking. I thought it was before, but with the heightened sense of hearing and seeing, it's so much better.

Going out as wolves together was strange at first, but it turned out to be like we've done this our whole lives—every move we made was in sync.

I never had anything as wonderful. Not to mention, those binds that connected Carter and I developed so strongly that I feel it in my soul and bones. He's the man for me, now and forever.

"Okay." I hadn't thought about it lately, but meeting his family formally would be a good thing. "How many more are there besides the ones I've already met?"

"You have some of their mates, the elders, about twenty-five or so single male wolves, and ten single female wolves."

A growl leaves me at the mention of the single female

wolves, and Carter smiles.

"You know you're the only wolf for me, baby."

"Better be." The wolf inside me snarls, baring her teeth. I have no doubt she'd take out anyone who came near Carter.

"We do have an Alpha bitch in the pack."

More growls come from deep in my throat, and my wolf pushes to get out. It takes everything I have to keep her at bay. "And this means ...?"

"Chances are, you'll be challenged."

"Challenged to what?"

"To fight, for me and for the Alpha position in the pack."

Anger bubbles. "Did you think of telling me this at any point in our conversations over the last few days, Carter?"

"Know you're pissed, but it's pack law. I can't change it or fight it. It's how we operate."

"So, you're telling me that I'm going to meet your entire family, who may or may not like me, then I'm going to have to fight some Alpha bitch to keep you and stay alive?"

"Yes."

He's way too nonchalant about all this.

I stand abruptly, my wolf seeming to take control. "This is shit, Carter. If you think for one second some woman wolf bitch is going to come and try to take you away from me and my life, you're sadly mistaken. Not to mention, I'm pissed as hell at you." With that, I open the door to the back deck, strip my clothes, and let my wolf run free. I've learned in this brief time that this is the best way to calm her—letting her run.

My wolf feels happy she could express herself through me. Even I feel better that it's out.

By the time I get back, Carter is on the phone. He ends

it when he sees me.

"Better?"

"I'm still pissed at you, but my wolf is better."

He stalks toward me and wraps his arms around me, pulling me to him. "You got this, Izzy."

"You want one of your wolves to die? You want me to have to kill someone?"

"She knows it's to the death, she knows. And if she doesn't want to take that risk, she will bow down and not challenge you."

"What about me? You're okay with me dying?"

"Fuck no. I don't want you to have to do this at all, but there isn't a choice."

"Aren't you Alpha? Can't you forbid it or something?"

"If I do that, it will make you come out as weak and my pack won't respect you. That isn't an option, Izzy. They have to know you, have to respect you, for this to work."

"I can't believe you're taking me to your family and I could end up dead and not come back home."

Carter growls. "No, you won't die. Your wolf is damn strong, and you can hack this. You need to trust in yourself and your wolf."

"How can you be this sure?"

"Because only Alpha female wolves can mate with an Alpha male. I've seen you out hunting."

My gut twists at thinking about the bunny and raccoon I took on and ate. Ew. Still not used to that part of being a wolf. She loved it. Me? The aftertaste made me a little nauseous.

"You'd better hope so, because if I die after becoming a wolf for you, I'm haunting your ass until you join me on the other side."

Carter laughs full-out. Asshole.

THE DEN IS HUGE. No other way to put it. I'm not sure what I expected, but a huge-ass house that looks similar to a hotel wasn't it.

As we enter a large, open room with couches and a television, all sounds stop. There must be fifty people in this room. Some I remember from the field, and a couple came to my house. Each of them have smiles for me.

"Alpha," Owen calls out with a wide smile on his face. "Izzy, so good to see you. And you're a wolf."

He doesn't come any closer, which I'm happy for. Something in my gut tells me that, if he got too close, Carter would pounce. I don't want that to happen with his family. I may be pissed at him, I may be getting into a hell of a fight today, or dying, but I don't want him not to have his family if I'm not here.

"Hi, Owen."

Introductions go around. I note some of the females give me sideways glances, but not one has stepped forward to "challenge" me. I take that as a good sign.

"Hi, Izzy." I turn toward the voice, and my heart drops as anger begins to bubble.

My realtor, Mr. Jacobs, and one of my lawyers, Mr. Simpson, stand there, hands at their sides. I can smell the worry coming off them. They should be worried. They so should be.

Without saying hi, my piercing gaze goes directly to my mate. "They're in your pack? The two people who did the paperwork on the house, the house that you *came with,* are in your pack? You set all this up!" I accuse as he comes near me, and I take a step back.

"Izzy, we're mates. I just had to make you see it."

"By screwing with me!" Fire burns like lava in my veins. I feel my wolf pushing to get out. Not that she'd hurt Carter, and I'm pretty sure I wouldn't be able to, either. However, I've never been a quitter and don't plan on starting now.

"You were human, Izzy. We had to get past that. Know you're pissed, but you'll get over it."

"Get over it!"

"Well, well, well, what do we have here?" a sultry voice to my left catches my attention, and my fury moves to her. She's beautiful in a way that she knows it, and I immediately peg her as the Alpha female.

"Izzy," I answer.

"I didn't ask your name, human," she retorts.

"Hate to tell ya, but I'm a wolf now."

She laughs. "Your wolf's so new she won't know what to do with a real wolf."

Inside me, my wolf snarls and growls, snapping her teeth repeatedly, begging to come out. It takes serious strength, but I keep her back.

"Ya think?" I retort, not moving from my spot. No way the bitch is going to make me lose my ground.

"Oh, I know." She pauses as she looks me up and down. "I challenge you ... for your mate." I growl as she looks at Carter and winks. "And position. You're dead, human."

Carter sighs. "Abbigail, you don't need to do this."

"Well, of course I do, sweetheart. You belong with me. In my bed, your cock inside me." She stares me down.

Something clicks inside me and my wolf takes control, pushing through. I feel my body changing in a flash. Abbigail's doing the same. Her wolf is dark brown to my almost white one.

As soon as we change, we circle each other, both growling and snarling.

Abbigail's wolf charges, swiping her claw at my face. My wolf pulls back just in time, but she nicks the edge of my nose. With that one cut, the background fades around me.

Abbigail's wolf comes at me again, this time her claws tearing into my shoulder. Inside, I feel that pain.

That's when my wolf fully takes over the fight. While I'm still present, her instincts are what's driving this. Her knowledge. She has full control, and as scary as it sounds, it feels good, because I know my wolf will protect us until her dying breath.

My wolf attacks, biting Abbigail's hind quarters. Pain comes to my left leg at the same time, and I feel blood trickle down. Somehow, my wolf shakes this off, and my already pissed off wolf goes ballistic.

She lunges, attacking in such a vicious way that I'm in awe. There is no delaying.

The taste of blood enters my wolf's mouth. She's hungry for, yearning, wanting more of it on her tongue.

My wolf grabs Abbigail by the throat and yanks, snapping the bones, and the taste of blood trickles down our throat. It does not taste good to my human half, but it does to my wolf.

My wolf relishes in the lifeless body of the one who dared challenge her. Me, I try to pull back from that. It's hitting me that I just took a life, and I'm not too sure I'm okay with that.

"Izzy!" Carter's voice comes through as my wolf goes for another bite and pulls, wanting to make sure the wolf is dead and no longer a threat. It takes him calling me two more times for me to pull through my wolf.

I change back, blood covering me. A T-shirt is thrown

over my body before Carter scoops me up in his arms. I'm too stunned to remember I'm pissed at him.

He takes me through The Den and into a room. Then I hear a shower turn on. He takes off my shirt, and seconds later, we are in the shower, where he sets me down and begins to wash me.

"I killed someone," I whisper.

"Izzy, that's the way of this world. We suffer losses just like everyone else. Like I said, she had a choice. She could have stepped back, but chose not to. It's not your fault."

"I'm not sure I can live like this, Carter."

"Hate to tell ya this, but you're in it now, baby."

My head falls to his shoulder as the warm water hits my back. A bubble of sadness comes up, and I let it out, releasing myself from it. Something inside me washes it away. It's like my wolf is taking over that particular feeling, knowing I can't handle it. I begin to feel free. The anger I had for him dissipates, as well.

Is this what being with Carter will be like? One minute we're pissed; the next calm? I think I can deal with that.

"Come on." The water is turned off, and then Carter carries me from the bathroom, grabbing towels on the way. He sits me on the bed and dries me, then himself. I'm not even sure when he took his clothes off.

My core clenches.

"I love you," I whisper.

He lays me down. "Love you so damn much, Izzy. We'll make all this work—you, me, the pack. Swear it. You're my forever."

Tears prick my eyes. "You're my forever."

Carter then makes love to me.

EPILOGUE

2 YEARS LATER

"THIS IS NOT NORMAL, CARTER!" I YELL AT THE TOP OF my voice while the doctor beside me chuckles. I extend my claws. "Do you want some of this?"

The doctor shakes his head nervously and moves out of the way. Like I couldn't get to him, please.

"Izzy, you're almost done."

"I've already squeezed two pups out! He"—I glower at the doctor—"said there were only two. Now, mysteriously, there are three! *No!*"

The pain hits, and my bottom half contracts repeatedly. It feels almost as bad as the sexual pains I had when I changed over from human to wolf. Only these end up with a child coming out of my body.

"Push, Izzy," the doctor instructs, and I do, with a growl.

Five pushes later, the third of our trio is in the world.

I lie back on the bed in a heap. Soft cries and snarls are heard throughout the room, and I look over to where they have my pups. My wolf inside growls, and I'm right along with her. I want my babies.

"Give me my babies now!" I order.

The three nurses carry them over to us. I snatch the two girls, and Carter grabs his boy. Then the nurses and doctors leave, knowing that us wolves are very territorial over our pups. Me especially. Apparently, I didn't get the cool down gene when it comes to my babies. No, anyone comes near them, I'll destroy them.

"They're perfect," Carter proclaims.

I take a moment to inspect them. Carter told me they wouldn't come out as wolves; that they'd be born human, but have the wolf inside them. I'm learning this whole wolf aspect of babies. Thank goodness for my computer skills. I've learned a lot.

"Yeah, they are," I whisper as my little girls burrow themselves into my chest. I look to my husband and mate, his face in awe of the little pup in his arms. He's going to be a fantastic father. That I have no doubts.

"What do you want to name them, Izzy? Know we've been going back and forth, but we never came to a decision."

"Caden for him."

Carter smiles big. That's the name he wanted for our boy, and I like it, so why not?

"Arianna and Sophia for these two."

"Perfect. This, Izzy, is what perfection is. Thank you for giving it to me. Love you."

"I love you, too."

Carter stands up and kisses my lips, making me fall even more head over paws for the man. Our life is perfect. This arrangement was the best thing that happened to the both of us.

EXCERPT OF THE ALPHA'S BARGAIN

The Alpha's Bargain (Howls Romance)
©Ryan Michele 2017

Chapter One

The wind whistled through the trees bending the strong trunks at its will. Leaves rustled creating music through the night's sky, while the clouds hid the moon leaving everything blanketed in darkness. The smell of rain lingered in the air everything indicating the storm was coming through, hard and fast.

Off in the distance, wolves howled warning of the fast approaching weather change.

My hair blew in the wind as the swing rocked back and forth watching the changes from my front porch. It was my favorite spot and spending hours here had become my past time. Whether the sun shone down, moon glowed or the storm rose, sitting here in this spot filled me with peace.

Storms were my favorite though, the more lighting, thunder and rain the better. It was as if two worlds were colliding bringing a force down on one another that rivaled the other. An epic battle of wills crashing and tearing through the land – all of it part of nature and her works.

Sporadically, the clouds would give way to the crescent moon playing hide and go seek with the earth below.

Small droplets began to fall to the ground, the dirt pressing out of its way before the water seeped in. A burst of energy floated through the air as lighting cracked, thunder crashed and the rain began to pour down around me. All the while not a drop hit me because of the large awning above.

The air invaded my lungs and the calm seeped deep into my body.

Yellow eyes glowed in the distance making their way quickly to me. A beautiful light brown wolf with white around his ankles hopped up on the porch, his nails tapping on the wood. He shook his body hard and fast spraying me.

Rolling my eyes, I wiped the wetness from my bare arms and glared down at my brother as he shifted. Ren, stood before me with a wide mischievous smile on his face. "Thought you could use a shower." He chuckled as a large crash of thunder hit shaking the ground beneath us, my feet feeling the long rumble.

"And here I thought I liked you."

Ren reached to the ground snagging his sweatpants and pulling them over his body. Wolves never cared about nudity. It's a part of our lives, but being siblings, my three brothers, kept themselves covered for the most part, which was greatly appreciated.

The swing gave a creak and groan as my brother's heavy

weight settled besides mine all the while the rain and wind picked up around us.

"Why do you love storms so much?" Ren asked pushing the swing back and forth with his powerful legs. Ren was the oldest in the family and would one day be alpha according to my father. A job that Ren rolled with and didn't make much fuss about. Stating, *he'd worry about it when the time comes.* Which to me was an admirable thing.

In some packs rifts would cause problems between the alphas fighting for dominance. So far, we'd skated those lines and hadn't had that issue.

"Peace Ren. In all the chaos that is the storm, the peace will come."

He let out a huge sigh and laced his fingers behind his head. "Have you told dad yet?"

My insides clenched and the headache that stayed at bay began to come back seeping into my temples. "No." Telling my father would mean trouble and bringing that to my family wasn't on the top of my list. The problem was it couldn't be hidden for much longer. We were drowning. Our pack, the one my father, his father before him and his father before him – grew was losing more money than we were bringing in.

Therefore, our savings was dwindling to the point of scraping by and no pack could survive the way things were. With sixteen mouths to feed, electricity that needed to be paid and to live, we needed a holy grail of help.

I'd done everything possible to get us back in the black and the stress of it has been getting to me and my wolf. Lately, she was restless to a point that a run nor a hunt would calm her. The human side of me wasn't much better. The pressure of making things right, of helping my family and not being able too was sending me down a dark path.

It couldn't be stopped because no matter what accounts money was shifted to or creative ways to put off the bills – they just kept coming. All of it weighed so heavy on my chest there were times I couldn't breathe and felt like an utter disappointment to everyone around me.

My parents had me attend the local Breed College and get a degree in finance, which only nailed my coffin harder because I felt like a failure on so many levels. The problem was the money wasn't coming in as fast as we needed to and it was time for everyone to get jobs outside the pack so we could get back on our feet.

Ren and I were the only ones who knew how low we were because I confided in him. It was either that or allow the pressure to take me completely under.

"We're going in now and talking to him, Caleigh. This can't go on and the longer we wait the further down we'll go."

He was right and the only reason for me putting it off was my ego which was totally stupid on my part. It was so damn hard though knowing you failed. You failed everyone around you when you should know exactly what to do to make it right. I had no other options at this point and finding a money tree wasn't an option.

"Right." I breathed not wanting to, but having to do the responsible thing. We rose from the swing just as another crash came to the earth. This time it felt like a warning, one that made the hair on the back of my neck stand to attention.

My father was the best man I knew, loyal, fair and trust-worthy to the highest degree. It was one of the reasons I was so down on myself about telling him. He put so much trust in me to handle the finances and here it was all fucked up.

Having him disappointed in me was the worst feeling

ever. Tears threatened to push their way to the surface, but I held them back and followed Ren into the pack house.

**

"I knew we shouldn't have renovated." My father looked down at the papers on his desk, his hands feathered through his dark hair and brow arched in worry. "That's what dragged us down so far."

He was right. Our pack owned two bars on the Breed side of town where the shifters resided. Each one gave a different feel to accommodate everyone. Howls was more upscale compared to The Grey Wolf where you'd find peanut shells all over the floor.

The Grey Wolf had been shut down now for four months for renovations that cost a mint. Alone Howls could hold its own and then some, but with The Grey Wolf shut down and the amount of money going out to fix the place up, we were falling.

"How much longer before Grey will be open?" I asked him hoping beyond measure he'd say tomorrow. Hope was a powerful thing.

"We have about two more months." He rubbed his hand over his face and sucked in breath. "Fuck, I don't want to go to the bank for a loan."

Breed had their own banks, but that wasn't the problem. The problem lay in other packs deeming you as weak because you needed to take out the money and not have it on point. Nothing was ever kept secret it seemed and word would get out that my father couldn't handle his pack or businesses. It would create a rift and look bad on all of us.

"I'm so sorry." I whispered feeling the ache in my chest grow tighter. The guilt of not hacking it rode me so hard it hurt like a physical pain squeezing the life out of me.

My father's head popped up. "What do you have to be sorry for Cal? You did everything exactly as it should be done. There are no *I's* or *T's* left uncrossed here. You've done nothing wrong."

My words came out in a choke, hearing my father, yet still feeling like a disappointment. "I let everyone down."

"Nonsense. It's just more money going out than coming in. It's business and you can't get all worked up because of it. I'll figure it out Cal."

"What can I do?"

"Right now, nothing. Give me some time and I'll get it worked out."

I had no idea how he would do this considering we were more than a hundred thousand dollars in the hole after moving it from savings, but he's my pack leader and I put my trust in him.

My father rose from his chair behind his desk. "Come here." I strode into his harms where he wrapped me in his warmth and kissed the top of my head. "Next time you bring this to me right away Cal and we'll figure it out."

I nodded.

"Love you."

"Love you too."

Find out more in The Alpha's Bargain HERE

ABOUT THE AUTHOR

Ryan Michele found her passion in bringing fictional characters to life. She loves being in an imaginary world where anything is possible, and she has a knack for special twists readers don't see coming.

She writes MC, Contemporary, Erotic, Paranormal, New Adult, Inspirational, and other romance-based genres. Whether it's bikers, wolf-shifters, mafia, etc., Ryan spends her time making sure her heroes are strong and her heroines match them at every turn.

When she isn't writing, Ryan is a mom and wife, living in rural Illinois and reading by her pond in the warm sun.

Join my Reader Group: Ryan's Sultry Sinners

Come find out more:
www.authorryanmichele.net
ryanmicheleauthor@gmail.com

OTHER BOOKS BY RYAN MICHELE

Ravage MC Series:
  Ravage Me
  Seduce Me
  Consume Me
  Inflame Me
  Captivate Me
  Ravage MC Novella Collection
  Ride with Me (co-written with Chelsea Camaron)

Ravage MC Bound Series
  Bound by Family
  Bound by Desire
  Bound by Vengeance

Vipers Creed MC Series:
  Crossover (co-written with Chelsea Camaron)
  Challenged

Conquering
Conflicted (Coming soon)

Ruthless Rebels MC Series (co-written with Chelsea Camaron):
Shamed
Scorned
Scarred
Schooled (Coming in July)

Loyalties Series:
Blood & Loyalties: A Mafia Romance

Raber Wolf Pack Series:
Raber Wolf Pack Book 1
Raber Wolf Pack Book 2
Raber Wolf Pack Book 3
Raber Wolf Pack Box Set

Standalone Romances
Full Length Novels:
Needing to Fall
Safe
Wanting You

Short Stories:
Hate to Love

Branded

Novella:
    Billionaire Up Romance
    Stood Up

www.authorryanmichele.net

HOWLS ROMANCE

Classic romance... with a furry twist!

Did you enjoy this Howls Romance story?
    If YES, check out the other books in the Howls Romance line!

The Werewolf Tycoon's Baby by Celia Kyle
    Grab more info on the Author's Website HERE.

Pregnant with the Werelion King's Cub by Claire Pike

The Alpha's Secret Family by Jessie Lane
    Grab more info on the Author's Website HERE.

The Billionaire Shifter's Secret Baby by Diana Seere
    Grab more info on the Author's Website HERE.

Royal Dragon's Baby by Anya Nowlan
    Grab more info on the Author's Website HERE.

The Werebear's Unwanted Bride by Marina Maddix
    Grab more info on the Author's Website HERE.

Hunted by the Dragon Duke by Mina Carter
    Grab more info on the Author's Website HERE.

The Billionaire Werewolf's Witch by Celia Kyle
    Grab more info on the Author's Website HERE.

The Wolf's Royal Baby by Milly Taiden
    Grab more info on the Author's Website HERE.

Her Scottish Wolf by Theodora Taylor
    Grab more info on the Author's Website HERE.

The Alpha's Arrangement by Ryan Michele
    Grab more info on the Author's Website HERE.

Falling for the Werewolf by Abbie Zanders
    Grab more info on the Author's Website HERE.

Her Unbearable Protector by Reina Torres
    Grab more info on the Author's Website HERE.

The Billionaire Dragon's Secret Son by Harmony Raines
    Grab more info on the Author's Website HERE.

The Big Bad Wolf's Ex by Tonya Brooks
    Grab more info on the Author's Website HERE.

The Alpha's Enemy Mate by Jessie Lane
    Grab more info on the Author's Website HERE.

EXCERPT OF THE RABER WOLF PACK

Raber Wolf Pack Book One ©Ryan Michele 2015

Prologue

Looking in the oval mirror of my great-great grandmother's vanity, I pucker my lips then smoosh them together, making sure the shimmery gloss is perfectly distributed. Swiping the excess off with my index finger, I focus on my eyes, checking that every single one of my long, mascara-covered lashes are in place. I hate clumps that make me look like a freak.

My ice-blue eyes are surrounded in a smoky gray shadow, and I used way too much eyeliner. Still, the effect turned out pretty hot, making my eyes the focal point of my face. A good thing considering I was initially going for the no-foundation look tonight, until the pimple on my chin told me that wasn't going to happen. I tried just covering the spot and blending, but it looked like a caked mess of shit and

I had to start all over. Of all the days for my face to blow up and sprout nastiness, it had to be today.

My best friend Masie had talked me into sneaking out of the house for 'the party of the year,' or so she called it. I'm weighing a lot on tonight. If my father catches me, I'm screwed. To say he's overbearing is an understatement. He's protective to the tenth degree and keeps me firmly under his wing, but I know he does it out of love. But, most of the time it sucks. He scares off every male wolf that comes around. With him being Alpha of our pack, I have yet to find a male that will stand up to him when it comes to me. No one has had the balls yet. Pathetic really.

The worst of it is, I'm horny. Seriously, I've gone without sex for way too long. Us wolves are sexual creatures and we crave that—no, *need* that release. I've masturbated so much I had to buy a new vibrator about a month ago. If I get laid at this party, it will be all worth it.

Sure, my father will yell at me if I'm caught, but that should be the bulk of it. He'll just be happy that I'm home and safe. So, I'm taking the risk.

The distinct smell of my best friend floats through the air. "Bitch, are you ready yet?" Masie calls from the doorway of the bathroom, peeking her head in, knowing she didn't surprise me. One great thing about being a wolf is our heightened senses—smell, hearing, and sight are extremely powerful. My father thinks we are hanging out over at Masie's house for the night and he's gone on pack business, so this works out perfect.

"I'm coming, wench, hang on." I run my fingers through my auburn hair. I added a few curls, which have softened into awesome cascading waves, flowing down to just above my waist. I give one more fluff before turning toward her.

"Fucking shit, Zara. Hello! Bitch in heat, here." She

waves her hand in the air, laughter ringing in her voice, and I can't help but join her.

"I am. Let's go." Hell yes, I am, no argument here. I stand, adjusting my clothes in the full-length mirror. My bright blue, tight-as-shit skirt stops mid-thigh, and my black chiffon see-through top hangs off my shoulder. Underneath, I'm wearing a very boob-flattering tank that pushes my girls up for maximum cleavage.

"Damn, girl, you have got to let me borrow that outfit. Not that my tits or ass would look as good as yours, but I want it." Masie has been my best friend since birth, and she has given me shit about what she calls my 'lush assets' since I got them. I have tits and ass, big whoop. It means nothing. Not in our culture. *Smell* is the only thing that matters. If the person looks good, that's a bonus.

"Maze, you need to stop with that shit. You are beautiful so shut the fuck up." Another line I've probably repeated about a zillion times over the course of our friendship. One thing that seriously pisses me off about my best friend is her opinion of herself. She's always finding something wrong, when there is absolutely nothing there. It's because she hasn't found her mate yet. She's twenty-three, like me, but all of her sisters—twenty-one, twenty, and nineteen—have already found their mates. With her being the oldest and not having found *the one*, it kills her inside. Masie thinks she has some defect that makes her scent unappealing. She's dead wrong.

Whenever we do go out, the males flock to her. They just don't have the scent she's searching for. And she looks hot tonight. Sexy black hair, sultry makeup. Her black skirt is the length of mine, but nowhere near as tight. Her long-sleeved top has cutouts on the shoulders, and a deep, plunging V in the front. It pushes her boobs up, too. I love it.

She may not find her mate, but there's no doubt she'll get some.

"I didn't see anyone else here when I came in," she states.

"Nope, all away on pack business. We are sleeping at your house. No harm, no foul," I reply, smacking my lips.

"All right then, let's go. We don't want the good ones to be taken."

Hell, even if they have already screwed a female, it doesn't mean they are done. Most male wolves can orgasm multiple times in the course of a night. Some can go multiple times in one session. Yes, please.

"After you." I grab my four-inch heels, black with shimmery blue at the very tip of the toe, and slip them on once we get down the two flights of stairs in my house.

Tonight is going to be one hell of a night.

Chapter One

Life is so fragile, even for immortals. One night was all it took for mine to change.

As pain surges through my body, I'm reminded of this very thing. Death would be better than this, but he won't end me. I'm too important to his master plan. I didn't want him to succeed, but as the months come and go in a blur of hurt and punishment, I feel myself doing the one thing I never wanted.

Breaking. Bending to his will.

On that fateful night I received my powers from the Heavens, when my Nana O told me that I was destined for great things, a higher purpose in this life, she didn't mean this. She couldn't have imagined that this would be my fate.

I scream as the man who is supposed to love me pushes a long, steaming hot, metal rod into my stomach. The smell of my burning flesh enters my nostrils and pain floods every cell of my body. I wait, hoping for relief, but even as he removes the rod, it doesn't come. If anything, it gets worse, more intense. The worst part of all of this is he can do this for the rest of eternity if he chooses. Death will never come for me.

No, Nana O could have never meant this.

Ian pulls me onto his lap, wrapping his arm protectively around me, as any mate should do. He even growls as one of the other wolves looks my way appraisingly. He should get an Oscar for his stellar performance. This one, though, is definitely above and beyond his call of duty. Nothing like my fake mate taking it to another level in order to impress.

Alpha Ty and his Beta, Gregor, sit at the long, sleek wooden table in the conference room. I call him Alpha because father is too nice of a name for him. The pack enforcers are seated around the table as well, as I sit with Ian off to the side by the far wall. Here, but not here. Observing, but not part of the meeting. Not that I want to be. I'd love to be far away from this place, but that's not an option for me.

A mediator from the Wolf Council, which Alpha pays off, sits at the head of the table to preside over this sham of a meeting. One to supposedly create an alliance between the two packs, but it's all a big façade. Nothing is as it seems, exactly like my life.

The Ren Pack sits on the other side of the table,

assessing each of our wolves, eyeing them with curiosity and suspicion. They should. Our Alpha has been calling meetings like this for the past couple of weeks, meetings that have only one conclusion—deaths, and none from our pack.

Wolf packs are slowly dwindling, becoming non-existent, because our Alpha is taking out the highest wolves from each pack. While he's here, the rest of the pack is at the Rens' compound, completely wiping them out, killing everyone there. Leaving no one to report what my Alpha is doing. No one to warn others. Our kind is slowly meeting its demise, all at the hands of *him*.

But that's what he wants. To rule. Have power. All it is, is greed plain and simple.

Alpha has always been power hungry, but only to the point of being the pack's alpha. Never, while I was growing up, did he ever give any indication that being Alpha wasn't enough. He was always around, teaching and prepping me for whatever my future might hold, and he always kept a close eye on me. He's made sure that I didn't stray too far from the pack. I thought that it was because he loved me. He was protecting me from all the bad in the world. But I was mistaken. Horribly so.

I sniff the air and notice a subtle shift from light and fresh to dark and musty. One of our wolves is seated next to the Ren alpha, his lip twitching, his nostrils flaring in and out. Low growls rumble through the air around us, thickening the tension in the space. I lick my lips and taste the change in the room. It's as if the once-breezy climate has swirled into a thunderstorm ready to erupt, and the warning reverberates through my body.

My pathetic job is to use my gift, my ability to listen to other wolves' thoughts, to find out if the Ren pack has reinforcements outside. Or if they even have a clue that they are about to be obliterated. Alpha looks over to me, brows raised expectantly. With a simple shake of my head, I silently feed him the answer he seeks. None of the other members of their pack are waiting outside; none of the men back at their home base have contacted anyone here for help, which means our other enforcers are cleaning up there. This is the moment I always dread. Each time I'm forced to do this, it's a hard, black strike against my immortal soul. The darkness claws at my insides, but I can't escape it. It's a mark that can never be erased. A scar that will never heal. I should never have been put in this position. Ever. I fear there will never come a time when I can come back from it.

"Challenge," Alpha calls out, and arrogance and smugness drip from that one little word. Inside the other Alpha's head is a mix of surprise and disdain, but no fear. Never show fear, that's what Alphas do. "Outside," Alpha declares, after a bit of a stare down.

They file out, leaving me alone with Ian and the Councilor. If we are anywhere outside of the grounds of our pack, Ian or someone is with me to watch my every move, like I'd even try to escape. I've thought about it, don't get me wrong, but there is no way out. The chains are too tight around my neck, tethering me to his will.

I'd rather be dead.

This is my life, my pathetic, miserable, unfulfilled eternity of life. I need to learn how to survive it because he told me he'd never allow me the peace of death. So, instead I am *mated* to someone who really can't stand me and have learned to accept being a pawn for Alpha and the pack. It's either survive and do as I'm told or... I shake my head from the thought as goosebumps rise on my skin. I can't go back there, I won't.

I say nothing as I sit, quietly waiting for it to all be over so we can go back home. I use the term *home* loosely. I'm required to stay with Ian on my parents' level of the main house. Ian and I share the same bed nightly and attend all pack functions together, including meal times. All packs believe that we are actually mates. I shake my head at the thought.

"I said I'd do it." My voice comes out raspy because my throat is so damn dry. I can't remember the last time I had water. My entire body aches, even my fingernails and the ends of my hair. It's been so long. So damn long.

"Take this." My father holds out a large yellow and orange pill. I stare at it, willing it to disappear. I just know that it's poison, but not the kind to kill me, the kind to torture me. "I said take it," he growls, less patient than a few minutes before.

I've already decided my fate. With a shaky hand, I reach out and take the pill from his outstretched one, careful not to touch his skin. He holds out a bottle of water and I take it hungrily.

"No!" he barks as I start unscrewing the lid, and I freeze. "The pill first, then you can drink the rest." I lift the pill to my dry, cracked lips, and place it on my sandpaper-like tongue. I press the water to my mouth and try to swallow the pill. I gag as it gets stuck in my throat, cutting off my air supply. "You stupid female. Drink!" he screams, and I do, dislodging the pill from my throat. I stare at him with the water still in my hand. I long to actually drink it, just to feel it going down my throat. That last sip didn't feel like anything but more pain. "What are you waiting for? Drink."

I lift the bottle with both of my trembling hands, afraid that I may drop it. I can't waste any of this water. I don't have any idea when I will get more and dehydration is eating at me. I down the contents in a hurried rush, my stomach churning with it. Way too much, way too fast. I fear that everything I just drank is coming up hard.

"You do not throw up," he orders and I choke down the bile forming in my throat. Please stay down, please stay down.

He leaves the room, only to come back a few hours later. I pray this will be the time that he lets me free. "You want to know what you just swallowed?" I don't want to know actually, but it is not really a question; he'll tell me anyway. "You now have a mate. With my pack. That pill will bind your scent to his, ensuring you smell like mates, and no one will dispute it. Now you can never fucking leave."

I want to cry, sob, and scream. I want to throw something at this monster. A mate. So, I'm stuck here. This can't be true. It just can't.

"Don't fight it, Zara. It's done," he says before turning and leaving the room again. I fall to the floor and curl into a ball, wrapping my arms around my legs. No...just no.

It's utterly disgusting the torture that Alpha continues to dole out on a daily basis. Like all of the other shit that he did to me wasn't enough.

The Councilor's eyes focus on us as Ian's hand trails up and down my thigh. I feel nothing. No spark. No want. No trembles. No tingles in regions that should have them. Ian's hot—longish blond hair, deep brown eyes, muscular frame—but he doesn't do anything for me. His smell is totally wrong and turns my stomach with each sniff. It isn't even slightly enticing, and the farther his hand goes up the more I want to vomit. Neither Ian nor I can smell the mating, just everyone else around us.

I push my wolf back down as she whines, shaking her head in despair. Aware of the Councilor's watchful eyes, I don't want him to sense the turmoil rolling around inside of me. My wolf is still very much present, but she has gone into a state of hibernation, only waking when it's necessary. Like at one of these meetings or when I'm required to shift with the pack. Other than that, I don't hear a thought or feel a movement from her. She only sleeps.

'Damn she's hot.' The Councilor has no idea that I can hear his internal dialogue. *'What I wouldn't give to fuck her.'* I clench my hands into fists, trying to block out his thoughts, but they keep coming at me, each one dirtier than the last. *'I'd bend her over, ass up high, face down, and pound that pussy until she howls.'*

My stomach rolls and vomit climbs up my throat. I choke it down. My only saving grace is that he can't utter a word out loud. If he did, Ian would have the right to rip out his throat. The bastard would do it too, just because he can.

'Done,' I hear Alpha voice inside my head as he speaks the same ones to Gregor. Since learning of my *gift,* as he calls it, I've learned how to tune in to one being and shut out the others around me. I've become so adept at hearing people that they don't even need to be in the same room for me to know what they are thinking. It comes and with Alpha, it's as if he has a direct link to me. Even hearing his thoughts, before he addresses anyone as he speaks.

Honestly, I can't stand it, or him for that matter.

"It's done. Let's go." I rise from Ian's lap, brush his hand off me, and move toward the door. Ian grabs my hand as I go. Gotta keep up pretenses, right? I don't fight it because... what's the use? I'm stuck.

The copper smell of blood infiltrates my nostrils as I step outside and walk through the massacred wolves lying on the ground. All six that were in the room are torn to shreds. Alpha and Gregor slip on their shirts and we head to the black SUV waiting for us. Clean up is for the enforcers to deal with later.

I climb into the very back, Ian by my side. Alpha and Gregor sit in the middle row while two enforcers take the front. I stare out the window, not saying a word, only here physically. I shut down all thoughts from others and try to find some kind of solace, but it doesn't come.

"You did good, girl." Alpha's praises mean shit to me. They are nothing but a pat on his back for another task done dutifully by me. I stopped caring the moment more wanting power outranked taking care of his family, his daughter. The coldness in his eyes that first time I rejected his plan still haunts me.

"Daddy, we can't do this," I plead, tears streaming down my face and crashing to the cold floor beneath me. I can't take someone's life just for the hell of it.

"You'll do what I fucking say or you'll stay in there," he barks, and my hands grip the metal slats of the cage he locked me in moments before. The space is small, and all I can do is either sit or curl in a ball. Wolves are not made to be confined. We are born to be free, roam free. This...this can't be happening.

"Why do you want to hurt the others? We have been so happy for so long." I appeal to his more human side, or at least I try. In all my years, he's never shown me this side of him. Angry, menacing, cold.

"You've no idea what is going to happen, but I do. You'll

work for me so it doesn't. You will do as I say or you'll remain locked in here."

A low whimper escapes my throat. Where's my mom, surely she wouldn't let him cage me up like this. Would she? And my brother? Where is he?

"Daddy, please," I beg, unable to stop the sobs this time, and my chest constricts with the thought of him leaving me like this. He can't.

"You made your bed." He turns off the light in the small basement room and walks out of the door, locking it behind him. Panic hits me like a boulder to the gut. No, please no.

I learned quickly that disobeying him would not be tolerated. I never in a million years would have thought my father could allow such deep greed to overtake him. That his pack would now fear him instead of respect him. I don't know him at all. The man I loved when I was a pup is dead and has been since I revealed my power. The only connection I have to this wolf in the vehicle with me is that he is my Alpha. Just as the man I once knew is dead, so is a piece of me. A part of me died inside that cage. I did what I could, but I couldn't stay locked in there.

"Thank you, Alpha." I keep my voice monotone, withholding any emotion. I placate him and give him what he wants; in turn, he and the others, except for my on-duty bodyguard, stay away from me on the property. Not that it's any better, but at least I have a sliver of peace and I'm not completely locked up.

"Only three more to go." A smarmy smile spreads across Alpha's face, menacing evil emanating from it. It's detestable and if I were powerful enough, I'd rip his throat out myself. Wolves honor their Alphas and treat them with the utmost respect, but I have no interest in that. To me, my Alpha has no honor. He doesn't deserve respect.

"Daddy, please no!" I scream loudly, the sound bouncing off the walls of the small room. The fear is so thick I swear I'm in a fog.

"You always were fucking stubborn. Do I need to bring your mother and brother back in here?"

I still and shake my head adamantly. The last time he brought them down here, he beat them while I watched. I screamed for him to stop, pleaded, but he didn't. My mother got it bad, but my brother, Zane, got it worse. At one point, I thought for sure he was dead, but my father brought in the healer and healed him in front of me.

"No...no..." I repeat, somewhat controlling the tremor in my voice.

"Are you ready to do as I say?" He stares at me with eyes that are so cold, I'm surprised ice doesn't form around them. No warmth. Void. Emotionless. Gone.

But I can't do what he wants me to do. I can't. "No."

"You are a stubborn fool." He's asked me the same thing every day for Heaven knows how long. I've held myself together, I don't know how, but I have. Unfortunately, part of me is beginning to crack. I feel it in my bones. Daily the fracture grows deeper, threatening to break. I'm terrified that the damage will be irreparable. What would happen then?

"One week. I'm calling the Raber Pack to set up a meeting with Xavier. They are tough so we need to be extremely prepared." Alpha's voice pulls me out of my treacherous memories. Ironic, the man who gave me the memory is the one to pull me from it.

Alpha and his men carry on conversations like this all of the time, like I'm not even in the van with them. I've learned a lot by listening, but it's not like I can do anything with the information. I file it all away, like everything else, just sitting there useless for another day.

"They are younger wolves so we'll need to double up on the enforcers when we ambush. We'll need the women, too. They'll need to help at their pack house," Gregor chimes in, like it's nothing in the world to take out an entire pack in the blink of the eye. True, our kind have been challenging each other for centuries, but not like this. Not this deceitfully and disgracefully. At least before, the wolves could hold their heads up high, with us, no way. Our heads should hang down in shame. Challenges were honorable and fair. This is flat-out murder.

"Zara, can you get a read on them before the meeting?" Alpha asks, turning around in the seat. His once-dazzling eyes that I loved looking into as a child now hold nothing but hate. I focus on his stare, not backing down.

"I've never seen them so I cannot conjure up their thoughts," I reply, with zero emotion.

"So, if we can get you a picture, can you do it?" he asks, hopeful.

"I've tried and it doesn't work. I have to physically see them in order to hear them." I have answered this exact question a slew of times and each time, it's the same answer. He knows my powers don't work the way he wants them to and I wonder why he continually asks.

"Shit," he growls. "Somehow we need to get her in contact with at least the Beta and Gamma. I don't want to chance her seeing the Alpha," he announces to everyone in the car, everyone but me. I find this statement a bit odd considering I'm around Alphas at his little meetings, but I could not care less. His reasons are his own and he'll never share with me. Maybe if I get close enough to the other pack they might rip my throat out and save me from this. Maybe then I could find peace.

"They have a decent-sized pack," Gregor states, rubbing his chin, deep in thought.

"I want as few wolves as possible around Zara," Alpha warns. I'd love to roll my eyes, but I don't. I sit here quietly. Even though I do his bidding, he never wants me around other wolves unless it's absolutely necessary. Because heaven forbid I find my true mate and try to leave the pack. I scoff at the thought.

Everyone thinks I'm mated to Ian. I played along at the ceremony, even bit him, but felt nothing—no cosmic electrical connection, or whatever is supposed to happen when wolves mate. It was only a bite. Other wolves stay away from mated females and since I took that stupid little pill, they keep their distance from me. I can't blame them. Somehow, it tricks them just like everyone else. The emptiness inside of me leaves little hope that my true mate is even in existence any more. I should be able to feel something, but instead there is nothing there for my true one.

"Meeting in my office after dinner and we hash this out," Alpha orders. "Zara, you're not needed at the meeting." Of course I'm not, not that I would want to go. His words just prove that I'm insignificant, a peon.

"Thank you, Alpha," I reply lamely, ready to go to my room and be alone. Ian may sleep in the same bed as me, but his stuff is elsewhere in the house. He tries to stay away from me any way he can, but that is just not possible. He has to keep up the farce for his own position in the pack.

His role used to be a low-level enforcer, and he was never going to move higher up in the ranks. So, at Alpha's request, *for the sake of the pack,* he mated with me. I really don't know the details of what happened between him and Alpha. What I do know is, Ian came out of that meeting pissed the hell off, but ranking under my father at number four in the pack. He's now Alpha's duty guard and mine as well. So began my life of un-blissful mating.

Chapter Two

We pull up to our massive compound, the driver nods at the gatekeeper and he opens the enormous metal gates for us to enter. Our pack has spared no expense regarding protection. The tall walls surrounding the property are made of concrete and have electric charges at the top. The home is huge, overdone, and not compatible with the way wolves are supposed to live. This is lush, eccentric, modern: straight lines and stainless steel and black everything. It is actually, not a home at all. It's a showcase. For who, I'm not sure. Only the wolves in the pack are allowed inside. It's not as if we're having parties and inviting everyone on the planet over to show it off.

The SUV stops and we pile out. I set off quickly in my heels, wanting to be alone, needing space. None of the males follow step and from Ian's thoughts, he's thankful that I'm leaving. As I enter the house, smells of roast beef fill the air, but it only makes my stomach twist. I try my damnedest to miss meal times, but my presence is requested so I must show, smile, and keep my mouth shut. I consume what my body will handle and leave as quickly as possible.

"Zara." My name being called from the kitchen as I step on the first stair toward my solace stops me in my tracks. My mother, the Alpha female of the pack. *Damn.* I once had the kind of mom that would bake cookies with you and fix your scraped knee. I had a mother that I could talk to about anything and everything. I had all of that and in the span of a few months, it disappeared. Of course, my father beat it out of her and no one in the pack stopped him. I could say it's not her fault, but I'd be lying. I do blame her. She was supposed to protect me. That was her job as my mother. Now, after all this time has passed, I feel nothing for her, not even in the furthest recesses of my soul, some minute space, it's gone. Her lack of protecting me is unforgivable.

"Yes, mother," I answer with the same tone I address anyone from my pack. Clean, respectful, to the point and with the least amount of words possible.

"Would you like to come into the kitchen and help me out?" Her cheerful tone does zip to change my feelings toward her. Inside her mind, she's squirming, trying to find some way to make up for what happened to me. Trying to find some way to get me back, to get me to look at her the way I did when I was a kid. News flash, it will never happen, not in this lifetime, which is a long-ass time.

"I'm rather tired from today's meeting. I feel the need to lie down," I reply, looking directly into my mother's eyes. *'I wish you'd forgive me. I'm so sorry, sweetheart. I wish things were different.'* Apologies flutter through her mind and she knows I can hear them, but I make it a point to not give her the satisfaction of a response.

With my mother being the Alpha female of the pack, she should exert that authority on me, but she doesn't. Alpha females, normally, rule every other female in the pack, but with us, it's different. While I'm respectful to her, she has so much pent-up guilt for not helping me that she allows me to do my own thing. Other females in the pack have noticed this, and my mother has been challenged because of it several times. But she won those battles, remaining the top female.

I also know that my father has commanded her to leave me be, but my mother would have done that on her own. It's another small reprieve. I have so few of them and I cherish each and every one.

"Sure. Dinner will be in two hours. See you then." She wipes her hands on a towel nervously, which is kind of funny when you really think about it. Alpha female, nervous? Whatever, I don't have the energy to think about it.

"Thank you, mother," I say as I turn and make my escape to my room. I lock the door, giving myself an ounce of privacy, not letting it faze me that every wolf living here has a key. I kick off my platinum heels, take off my light gray skirt, and white blouse. I throw on my comfortable clothes, black yoga pants, and an old *Margaritaville* t-shirt. I enter my attached bathroom and avoid my eyes in the mirror. I just can't. When I look at myself, I have to face what I've helped Alpha do. It's better to keep avoiding it. Keep feeling nothing.

I grab a cleanser wipe and scrub all the makeup off my skin. I brush my teeth, trying to rid the bad taste today left in my mouth, and then twist my hair up into a messy bun, pulling a hair tie around it.

I fall into the bed and look up at the ceiling. Quiet, peace. All the voices are turned off, nothing clouding my head, leaving only me.

I royally suck.

I had such high expectations for myself. Such high

hopes. My parents were overprotective but not horrible while I was growing up. I thought I'd meet my mate and there would be this instantaneous, heart-stopping moment where we would be the only ones in the whole world. That everything would pause and the only focus would be on our connection. I had visions of my heart beating in sync with the man I was supposed to be with and talking to him through the mating link. I wanted that connection and more importantly, I wanted love. That absolute, unconditional love that only exists in human fairytales. Yep, that kind of love.

I was going to have a claiming ceremony filled with love and devotion. We would mark each other and be together until the end of eternity. We would have lots and lots of hot sex that would result in a ton of pups running around and be...happy. I'd be happy.

Instead, I am this. A shell of the strong, independent, take-no-shit-from-anyone woman that I used to be. I loved those things about myself. I was proud of them. I had confidence and even thought I was pretty. I had ambition and dreams.

It's amazing how all of *me* was destroyed. Now, I'm nothing. Alone. With each day that passes, I chastise myself for trusting him. Distressing thoughts constantly flitter through my head. Unable to stop them when I'm asleep, nightmares consume me. If only he would have given me death, then I could at least have peace.

The emptiness in my soul tightens, and knots form in my gut. What's left of my failed heart shrinks more and parts chip off, swirling into the abyss of nothingness. The hope that I once held so dear is shredded and set aflame, dissipating forever. Wetness forms behind my eyes. I will not cry. I will not shed one more damn tear on the poor, pitiful me train. I choke it back and breathe in deep, fighting the emotion with everything I have.

I look up at the ceiling, counting the intricate circles that someone took so much time painstakingly engraving into the worn ceiling. No one in my pack probably even notices. But they have become a lifeline for me these past months. Counting them one by one in order to get away from all of the thoughts in my head, those of mine and those of others. Counting, slow and methodical, until my eyes begin to close and I drift off.

Tired. Alone. Caged. Constricted. Restricted. Hopeless.

A sharp clang rings out. Steel metal bars encase me from top to bottom, leaving only a cold metal floor, where I lie naked. I jolt from the noise. Please not again. Please not again. I've been holding on to what little sanity I have left for quite some time. How many days, I have no idea. They all blend together at this point.

Stubborn, my father calls it. Disrespectful. Unappreciative.

"Get your ass up," he yells into the cage. I try to obey, but my body is so weak, so tired. It takes a bit, but I push myself up on my hands and knees, panting with each move. Not having regular food and water, especially when you're a high metabolism wolf burning food faster than one can consume it, is disastrous. I rise to my feet, ever so slowly, legs trembling from holding my weight as I grasp onto the metal bars.

"Why are you doing this to yourself, Zara? Why put yourself through this? Just say yes and all of this will be over." My father's voice echoes throughout the room.

I can't give up. There is still hope, hope that my father

will see that he is wrong. He wants me to be his puppet. I can't be part of that. I don't want anyone killed.

"So, what is it today? Yes, you'll do what I say, or no and you're still trapped?" Being trapped is horrendous. Being trapped in this confined space is inhumane. And the male standing before me that was supposed to love me uncondi-tionally, did this to me. He left me to rot in my own feces and piss. I will not let him win.

"No." My words come out croaky from lack of water and little to no saliva coating the inside of my mouth. My body is changing. What once was curves and luminous skin is now dull and bony. My hair. My beautiful hair. Chunks of it have fallen out, fluttered to the filthy ground.

"Fine, suit yourself." My father picks up a metal rod. I've never seen it before and have no idea what it is. Panic and fear paralyze me. He picks up the end of it and electric currents wiggle back and forth from two spikes coming out of the sides. Holy shit. "You did this to yourself, and you have no one to blame but yourself."

The rod inches closer and closer. I try to move to the corner of my small box to escape, but there is no use. The rod pierces me...

Ahh...holy shit. I wake with a start, sitting up on the bed and looking around to make sure I'm not *there*.

Bed. Curtains. Vanity. Bathroom. Check.

My heart is racing and I will it to slow down by breathing deeply. I'm fine. I'm not there any more. I'm not in physical pain any more.

I wipe my hands over my face and thread them through my hair. Nightmares. I have them every time I close my eyes and try to fall asleep. They come at me like a raging bull over and over again, knocking me on my ass each time, and leaving me back in that place. I wish I could wipe it from my head, make it go away just for one night of peaceful sleep.

It doesn't surprise me that I zonked out. I hardly sleep at all now. Usually, only when I'm so exhausted that it pulls me under. I hate sleeping because it leads to dreams and each time I wake up from one, I hate my father more. I hate him with every cell in my body. I hate what he has become. What he has made me.

My hands start to throb and I realize I've balled up the blankets on my bed and am squeezing them hard enough for my knuckles to turn white. I quickly release them, not wanting to rip the fabric, and thanking the Heavens that my claws didn't extend.

Inside, my wolf cries. When I was captured, she came out fighting, but my father shot me full of tranquilizers, debilitating my wolf and not allowing her to come out. As time went on, the tranquilizers were cut and my wolf's restlessness was making me even crazier. At one point, I thought the tranquilizers would be better than having an ill-tempered wolf clawing at my insides. Also, I had yet to hone my skill of reading minds and voices swam in my head constantly. Between that and my wolf, I was losing it. I'm not sure how I did it, but I willed my wolf down. She's stayed down for the past two years.

I look to the clock and only forty-five minutes have passed since I lay down. What I wouldn't give for a full night of restful sleep. I sit up on the bed and pull myself together.

"Open up," Ian bellows from the other side of the door, hitting it with his fists for good measure. I jolt from the sound. Damn, must be dinnertime. I open the door and meet his pissed-off face. "Are you ready?" he barks, eyeing me with disdain. He's told me many times that he's pissed he'll never find his true mate because of me. I sat there quietly during his words, but what I wanted to tell him was at least he had a choice in the matter. He's the one that agreed to do this to move up in the ranks. He could have taken a different route, but I kept my mouth shut because my words would have just added fuel to his fire, and I was not going to deal with him.

My mask falls into place. "Yes, of course." He holds out the crook of his arm and I place mine through the hole, hating even touching him.

'*I cannot believe I am stuck with this shit for the rest of my life. Being by her side. What the fuck? Like my mate isn't out there. All this shit had better be fucking worth it.*' His thoughts ring in my ears. He knows I can hear them, but he long ago stopped giving a shit. He can think what he wants; at least my thoughts are my own. No one can have those.

We enter the main dining room where rows of tables and chairs sit, along with a huge buffet full of food. No one utters a word to us as Ian lets go of my arm and we get in the buffet line. I gather some lettuce, tomatoes, cheese, and crackers and walk over to our spot at the table. This is not a *come sit where you want and be comfortable* room. No, this is a formal, *sit in your spot, no questions asked* kind of room. Ian slides in next to me, his plate loaded with meats, and my stomach rolls. I push my fork into the lettuce, then place it in my mouth and try to choke some of it down. I'm not sure what happened to me all of that time I was locked up, but something inside of me changed. From when I got out and to this day, I have a very difficult time keeping anything down.

A plate is slid in front of me from the other side of the

table. Roast beef. "Eat that. You haven't been eating right," my mother states like she actually gives a damn. She didn't care for years and now she wants to care.

"Yes, Mother," I say respectfully and pull the plate in front of me, even though my stomach protests. I force down the entire plate, wiping my lips when I'm finished. My body immediately wants to expel the food, but I do my damnedest not to let it.

Conversation carries between the wolves. None of it involves me so I don't bother listening. Anyway, if I wanted to know, I could go into their thoughts and find out. But I don't care. Alpha sits at the head of the table with my mother at his side, ever the stoic wife. They make me sick, pretending to be a happy couple. I can smell they are mates, but I've always wondered if my mother had a choice, what would she choose? It doesn't matter.

"So, did you hear?" Lisa, a female wolf, states loudly from the other side of the table as I go back to my salad. Why her voice catches my attention, I don't know. Normally I tune everything out. "Melody found her mate!" she squeals. My food rumbles again. I swallow. Mate. The hollow black abyss of my despair opens wide, swirling like a tornado threatening to suck me in. There have been so many times when I wished it would, but it doesn't, only leaving me with an ache so deep inside my chest that it's physically painful.

'Hopefully that little bitch heard that.'

Lisa's thoughts come through loud and clear. She's always been a bitch, but since Ian decided to tell her that we are not really mates, she is an even bigger one. When he told me, I stood there shocked as hell. He must trust her to give away that big of a secret because if Alpha finds out, I'm sure Ian will be dead.

Lisa hasn't yet mated with anyone, but she finds it prevalent to discuss these things at the dinner table, knowing and liking that it gets to me. After all the excited yelps from the pack, things settle down.

"Did you hear that?" Lisa states and I don't look up; surely, she isn't talking to me. "Hello, Zara I'm talking to you," her catty voice calls out. I breathe in deep, not allowing any emotion to seep through.

"Yes, Lisa. That is wonderful news." I dig into my salad and put a bite into my mouth, praying it will go down.

"Isn't it fantastic that everyone is finding their true mates?" She claps her hands in rapid secession, happy as all get out. '*Suck on that one.*'

Boy I'd love to lay into this bitch and tear her throat out. I'd never get that far though. I'd be pulled away because I'm too *useful*.

"Yes, it is." And isn't it sad that you haven't found yours, you conniving piece of shit.

"Melody is already planning the claiming ceremony and it's going to be grand." Oh sweet Heavens, here it comes. "You'll be there, right?" Like I could be anywhere else. Melody is a member of our pack and one of Lisa's many followers. Too bad she's losing one of her minions. Also too bad that if she joins whatever pack her mate is in, the family she grew up with will probably wipe her out. Pathetic.

"That will be up to Alpha," I reply in the same damn tone I hate.

"You will be required to attend," Alpha states from the end of the table. No doubt he wants to rub the mating in my face, too. Show me just how wonderful it would be to have found my true mate. He's made me go to all of them since agreeing to his terms. Each time, I just stand there, and then

I leave as soon as I'm allowed. I suck it all in, but never allow anything on the outside to show.

"Thank you, Alpha. I will be there, Lisa." She squeals again like a pig in a puddle. Inside, I'm rolling my eyes. Outside, I'm blank.

"Great, maybe Alpha will *let* you help out." '*Make you suffer some more, you bitch.*' Suffer. Didn't I already do enough of that? I have no mate to find. I have nothing. I *am* nothing. So why put me through more of nothing when I don't give a shit. I never got hate from my pack growing up. It didn't start until I got out of the cage and no one said a word to me as to why. I didn't even bother to ask or dig in their heads because I was past the point of caring.

"She will not be able to. She has work to do," Alpha announces. I don't know what's worse, doing his *work* or being around a bunch of giddy girls as they are decorating for a celebration and all the while rubbing salt in my gaping wound. Kind of a tossup really.

I say nothing. When Alpha excuses himself from the table taking Gregor, Ian, and some others with him, I leave, keeping my eyes focused ahead on the exit. I slam the door, run to my bathroom, and everything in my stomach makes its way into the toilet. I allow the tears to fall.

Read more in The Raber Wolf Pack HERE

Made in United States
North Haven, CT
13 October 2022

25369204R00082